IDENTITY

CRISIS

MELISSA SCHORR

MeritPress | fw

Published by
Merit Press
an imprint of F+W Media, Inc.
10151 Carver Road, Suite 200
Blue Ash, OH 45242. U.S.A.
www.meritpressbooks.com

ISBN 10: 1-4405-9013-3
ISBN 13: 978-1-4405-9013-9
eISBN 10: 1-4405-9014-1
eISBN 13: 978-1-4405-9014-6

Printed in the United States of America.

10 9 8 7 6 5 4 3 2 1

Cover design by Stephanie Hannus & Sylvia McArdle.

This book is available at quantity discounts for bulk purchases.
For information, please call 1-800-289-0963.

DEDICATION

For Alexa & Charlotte

ACKNOWLEDGMENTS

I was standing, oh so appropriately, in the middle of Disney World when I received the magical words from Jacquelyn Mitchard that she wanted to publish this book, so, yes, dear reader, dreams can come true. Thanks to her and the whole team at Merit Press, including Deb Stetson, publicity manager Bethany Carland-Adams, designers Stephanie Hannus and Sylvia McArdle for the beautiful cover, and Skye Alexander for the keen copyedit. Thanks to my savvy agent Jackie Flynn, who was willing to take the leap with me into a fresh new partnership. And of course, a shoutout to the inspirational Stephanie Gertz, whose invitation led to a chance conversation with Meredith O'Hayre, who made it all happen.

Time is a writer's most precious resource, and Justin Ahern, Deb Dunn, and the Noepe Center for Literary Arts on Martha's Vineyard gave me a pinch-me-I-must-be-dreaming gift—a glorious week in August on the Cape to complete the manuscript, alongside a talented group of children's writers. I am also fortunate, after irrationally holding out for so long, to have landed in the critique group I did, with the amazing moral support and sharp feedback from Monica Tesler, Marilyn Salerno, Julia Flaherty, Lisa Rehfuss, and Debbie Blackington. Thanks to Rebecca Fredey for serving as my honorary teen beta reader. And a shout out to my supportive colleagues at the *Boston Sunday Globe Magazine*, who graciously let me wear two writing hats.

Much love to the entire Cohen clan: my in-laws Jeff and Maureen, Eric, Brian and Dan, and my sanity-saving sister-in-spirit Stephanie Cohen. And always, to my supportive family, my exceptional mom, Thelma Grossman, and my dearly missed dad, Seymour, whose warped sense of humor lives on in everything I write. To my two dazzling girls, Alexa and Charlotte: Thank you for letting me keep pursuing my dream, and may you always keep pursuing yours. And forever gratitude, a second time, to my husband Gary. Even when I lost faith, you always believed.

CHAPTER 1

ANNALISE

Cooper Franklin thinks that just because I'm staring at the clock on the wall, I didn't notice him sneak a peek at my boobs. But I did. I totally did. Didn't anyone ever teach this boy the concept of *peripheral vision*?

I half-want to call him on it and give him a piece of my mind, but I decide I better not. Ms. Pinella, our tenth grade math teacher, has just partnered us up for today's lesson on probabilities, reaching into her bag of teacher tricks for a gimmick guaranteed to get our attention—especially during fourth period, the last class before lunch.

Sheer bribery.

She'd tossed each team an unopened package of M&M'S and told us to start by tallying how many of each color are in a given bag. For a nanosecond, it feels like an end-of-the-year party, especially when loudmouth Tyler Walters calls out, "Can we eat the candy afterwards?" and Ms. Pinella laughs, "Yes—so long as you get all the answers right." Then, naturally, she hands out a worksheet full of mind-numbing questions:

1. When you open a bag of M&M'S, what is the probability your first piece of candy will be tan?

2. Brown or red?
3. Not yellow?

Ooof. Way to crash a sugar high.

Cooper grabs the bag, full of enthusiasm, and starts sorting the candy into little piles on his desk, while I flip open my notebook, ready to mark down how many of each color we have.

Still, there's no way my brain can concentrate because in T-minus five minutes, concert tickets will go on sale to the all-time, most awesome rock band, ever, ever, ever, to hit the States, since the Beatles, the Rolling Stones, and the Sex Pistols combined. I'm talking, of course, about Brass Knuckles, who will be playing Boston's Agganis Arena two weeks from today in their first-ever U.S. tour. And even though my mom swore up and down to Sunday she wouldn't forget to call Ticketmaster right at noon today, do I trust her? No way, José Olé. Not with something this essential. I secretly programmed an alert on her iPhone, with an alarm set to go off exactly . . . three minutes from now.

Tick-tock. Tick-tock.

My eyes are Super Glued to the regulation black-and-white clock up on the wall, watching the sweeping second hand count down to the moment when those golden tickets are safely mine. I can imagine myself at the concert, singing along with 10,000 other Knucklies to the lyrics of their breakout hit, "Identity Crisis."

"You see me, Baby
And I see you
But perception can be so untrue
I'm having an . . . identity crisis
Why'd you have to leave me to my own devices?"

I can't stop fantasizing about The Moment. It's Viggo Witts's trademark move; I've watched him do it in countless YouTube videos. He strolls into the audience, plucks one lucky girl out of the crowd, pulls her on stage, and serenades her. Then, they sing the last chorus together, as a duet. Not like my voice would ever get me voted the next American Idol, but who cares? When I'm at that concert, Viggo will look out into the sea of girls, just know I'm his most devoted fan ever, and choose me. He'll lead me on stage, and even though we'll be watched by an arena full of people, it'll feel like it's just the two of—

"Bradley!"

I jerk at having my daydream so rudely interrupted. I realize Cooper has just said something to me—and I have no idea what.

"Hel-lo? Annalise Bradley, are you there?" Cooper is peering at me. "That's seven yellows," he repeats patiently, pointing to a pile of yellow M&M'S on his desk.

"Sorry," I sigh. Sad but true, I am here, not where I really I want to be: in a private jet with Viggo and the guys, who I happen to know from following their tweets are flying down to San Fran for tonight's show right this very minute. "Seven yellows." I jot it down in my neatest handwriting, which isn't exactly all that neat.

"Ten blues. Eight oranges. Got that?"

"Got it." I make a big point of tilting my notebook in his direction so he can see for himself.

Pleased to finally have my undivided attention, Cooper grins at me, patting his belly. "I'm starving. Think Pinella would notice if I—" he scoops up the small pile of red M&M'S and cups his hand toward his gaping mouth.

"Cooper, come on!" I shriek, pressing my fingers into his arm, which I can't help but notice is more muscular than I'd expected. "We haven't finished counting those yet!" I'm pretty sure he's just messing with me, but I can't take the chance. I'm not some numerical savant like Little Miss "Brainiac" Noelle Spiers over there, and don't want to blow this assignment because he's having a mid-morning snack attack.

"Kidding, Bradley. Jeez." He laughs and gently spills them back onto the desk. "Although, if I were to eat just one, it would be . . . this one." He plucks out a green M&M and holds it lasciviously between his thumb and index finger. He leans toward me, close enough that I get a whiff of something sickeningly sweet. Cologne? Conditioner? Raging pheromones? "You know what they say about the green ones, dontcha?"

I can't help but snort, half in laughter, half in disgust. "Funny." I roll my eyes at him. Cooper is cute and all, with his wavy brown hair and green eyes and Zoom-brite smile, but he totally knows it, which kind of cancels it out, in my opinion. Elementary math, right? And I still haven't forgiven him for the sneak peeks, either.

Not like that makes him any different than all the infantile boys at Dansville High. Chest-obsessed, every single one of them. Ever since I developed these darn "floatation devices," as Tyler Walters chortled at Amanda Gerard's pool party the summer before seventh grade, the entire male species has treated me differently. Oh, sure, their mouths still talk to me, Annalise Bradley—five-four, curly reddish hair, hazel eyes—but inevitably, their eyes slip southward, as if my brain is too dumb to notice.

The guys—and honestly, even the girls—at my school all assume that just because you look a certain way, you act that way too. Which is So. Not. True. It's not like I vamp around in V-necked rhinestone bustiers like a Real Housewife, or post multiple selfies of me in a bikini daily, like the desperates in one of Tori D'Fillipo's online beauty contests. No, every morning, I cram myself into a curve-flattening compression bra from Macy's, like I'm Mulan trying to pass for a Chinese warrior, and slap a Knucklie T-shirt and a hoodie on top. Still doesn't matter. The rumors that spread about what happened between me and Amos Landry at last year's Freshman Fling didn't help any, that's for sure.

Thank god for my best friend, Maeve, who's model-tall and string-bean skinny. She says that boys are just pigs and girls are just jealous, and that if she had my boobs, she would use them for world domination.

"Final tally?" Cooper asks, crumpling up the empty M&M'S bag and shooting it at the wastepaper basket in the corner without Ms. Pinella noticing. Score.

I point at my notebook.

Yellow: 7
Blue: 10
Orange: 8
Red: 7
Tan: 5
Brown: 7
Green: 10
Total: 54

As we get started on the worksheet, I can't help but sneak another peak at the clock over his head. It's a quarter after already. What's *taking* my mom so long? Could she still be on hold? I'd told her to have Ticketmaster send me a confirmation text so I'd know the instant the deed was done. But my phone's in my pocket set to vibrate, and hasn't so much as made a twitch.

"What's with the time check?" Cooper asks, tracking my gaze to the dial face. He arches an eyebrow at me. "Secret fourth-period rendezvous? Should I be jealous, Bradley? I thought this was *our* special time."

"Puh-leeze." A jock like Cooper wouldn't get it. Sports is his thing, not music. He'd probably mock Viggo's signature blue streak in his bangs, or Teen Heart Throb status, or how he got his start on the Disney Channel when he was eight, like most haters. Cooper probably still listens to Kanye. Or, worse, country.

The room fills with the sound of pencils scratching on paper and low murmurs. As Cooper and I work through the answers, heads tipped together and whispering softly, I can feel eyes boring into the back of my head. I glance over my shoulder and, sure enough, from two rows behind me, Eva Winters is giving me her trademark death stare, the one she's perfected just for me. Brrrr. I quickly turn away.

After about fifteen minutes, Ms. Pinella comes around to collect our work, reviews the answers, and gives us all permission to chow down on the leftover candy during the last few minutes of class. Cooper offers me some, but I shake my head. As if I'd really want them, after his grimy boy hands have been all over them. Not to mention I've lost my appetite. A pit is beginning to grow in my stomach. Still no word. How could my mom blow this simple assignment? I am dying to text her for an update, but I know if Ms. Pinella even catches me checking my phone during class, she'll confiscate it for the rest of the day, and I can't take the risk. I'll just have to wait until class is over to find out.

I sit there, antsy, distracted, willing the bell to just ring already, *ring!* as Cooper pops a handful in his mouth, savoring the taste of dissolving milk chocolate. He plucks another one, tan this time, holds it up, and looks me dead on in the eye. "Ever think how much M&M'S reflect humanity?"

I look at him warily. Where is he going with this? I'm really not in the mood for another dumb horny guy joke.

"We may come in different colors on the outside, but underneath?" He thumps his chest twice and makes the peace sign. "We're all the same."

Inwardly, I have to sigh. Cooper is relentless. Ever since we ended up as seat mates in math this year, he's been doing verbal backflips to get my attention, and I'm pretty sure I know why. But I'm not falling for some wannabe homeboy's charm act. Not again.

"Wow, Cooper," I say. "You are soooo deep. Like, Grand Canyon worthy. I had no idea."

Cooper puts on a face like he is actually wounded. "You know, Annalise, you have no idea of a lot of things about me."

"Oh, really? Illuminate me." I cross my arms. "Tell me your deepest desire, Cooper Franklin. Your innermost thoughts." This ought to be good. Amused, I pop a piece of candy in my mouth and lean back to enjoy the show. I have no illusions. When it comes to Cooper, what you see is pretty much what you get.

Clearly, my challenge has put him on the spot. He opens his mouth, grasping for what to say. "Well—"

Before he can finish his thought, the bell rings. Freedom! I zip to my feet and sling my backpack over my shoulder. "Maybe next time," I say, tossing the words behind me as I race into the hallway and pull out my phone. I need to text my mom right now and find out what's going on with those tickets. I may not know Cooper's deepest desire, but I definitely know my own.

CHAPTER 2
NOELLE

Even though nothing Eva does should shock me by now, I still honestly can't believe her sometimes. She invites herself over to my house after school, with Tori, naturally, in tow, sprawls dramatically across my canopy bed, and announces, "Did you see how that skank Annalise was, like, throwing herself at Cooper all through math class? It was disgusting. She was all, 'Oooh, Cooper, you are so funny. Oh, Cooper, you are soooo deep. Oh, Cooper, I want to scarf down green M&M'S with you.'"

Tori, the only one of our threesome who wasn't with us in class, because she's in remedial math—which we all know, but never mention—stops unwrapping the new lip plumper I'd just tossed her and turns to me sympathetically, as if to say *seriously?*

Then the two of them inspect my face, trying to gauge how upset I look. Even among my two besties, I hate being the subject of scrutiny like that. Hate it. Which Eva, of all people, should know. I try to tell her it wasn't that big a deal, but it's no use. Eva and Tori also know my dirty little secret that's unfortunately crystal clean. That I've been in love with Cooper Franklin forever.

"Yes it was," Eva says, indignant I dared contradict her. "You should have seen her giggling and squeezing his muscles. You were all the way on the other side of the room, but I was right behind them. I heard the whole thing."

She's right about one thing. Even from three rows over and two seats up, I can tell that Cooper's into Annalise. He's always stealing glances at her while we're supposed to be doing the problem set—just like I do at him. It's been like that since we all ended up together in fourth period math this year, either by fate, total randomness, or because some computer program has a wicked sense of humor.

I'm not sure Eva's right about Annalise, though. She doesn't seem *that* into him. Today, she was staring mostly at the clock on the wall, like she couldn't wait to get out of there. But Eva's what my English teacher, Mr. Charles, calls an "unreliable narrator": a person telling a story that you really can't trust, like the creepazoid in the book we just finished, *Lolita*. She's had it out for Annalise ever since what happened last year with Amos. Even now, she puts a slutty spin on every move that girl makes.

Eva must have read my mind, because she brings up his name. "First Amos, now Cooper. Someone has to keep that girl's claws out of Dansville's entire male population." She hops off my bed with an evil gleam in her eye, the same one that convinced Tori and me to cut class last spring and head into the city for a daytime *Divergent* marathon. The same one that got us busted when Tori's mom found her ticket stub in her jacket pocket. Usually, I envy Eva's bravado, something I totally lack. But not when it gets me grounded for a week.

Eva settles into my desk and starts tapping away at my laptop, suddenly shouting, "Noelle! Oh. Em. Gee!" so loud Tori practically smears the lip gloss across her perfect upper lip.

I rush over to the screen, freaked she's discovered a virus about to fry my hard drive or some Net Nanny monitoring software my parents have secretly installed. But no. She's just pulled up Annalise's profile and is scrolling down through her friends, photos, favorite books, movies, TV shows, and music, where there's just one artist listed: Brass Knuckles, with a link to their fan site. Well, duh. Anyone with half a brain can't help but notice how Annalise cycles through a different Knucklie T-shirt every week, plasters their photos all over her notebook like she's in middle school, and talks about them incessantly.

Eva whips around and scolds me. "I can't believe you're still friends with her! You traitor!"

Clearly, I'd missed the memo that I was supposed to defriend Annalise after the "Amos incident." But I dreaded the defriending process. What if someone noticed and called you on it? Confrontation is not my thing. Besides, I don't have over a thousand contacts like Eva, who friends every person she's ever met—and even more she hasn't. Or Tori, who's practically an Internet celebrity, with a zillion tween followers from her weekly beauty pageant, *InstaHotOrNot*? When you have a measly 151 friends like me, every one counts.

I mutter something about forgetting to get around to that, not sure when I'd even friended Annalise to begin with. At the beginning of freshman year, probably, when the three middle schools in Dansville merged into Dansville High. Those first few weeks, things were fluid and everyone was still super-friendly to everyone, until you looked around and suddenly cliques had hardened into place, just like the chocolate dip on a Dairy Queen ice cream cone that starts all gooey then an instant later turns into a shiny candy shell.

Eva shoots me a look and says, "Well, I guess I can forgive you since it's going to work to our advantage." Tori drops the lip plumper and strolls over to the computer, curious what Eva is up to, and Eva turns to both of us and smirks mischievously. "Like I said, something needs to get her distracted from Cooper. Something like . . . an online romance!"

Tori laughs cautiously, asking with who, and Eva replies, "With nobody! With someone we invent. The perfect guy. Someone cute. Someone she has so much in common with they are meant-to-be. Her soul mate. A Brass Knuckles fanboy! And, someone who lives far away, so they have to do the long distance thing." I see the familiar determined look in her eye and realize she is dead serious. I secretly believe everybody, whether they know it or not, has a defining motto, a principle by which they live their lives. Eva's would be: *only boring people get bored*. She's the original Drama Queen, even if she has to occasionally create her own.

"We can't do that!" I object, thinking how wrong that would be. Not like I have much sympathy for Annalise, after what she did to Eva last year. And watching Cooper flirt with her every day for the last couple weeks feels like being stabbed in the gut, Caesar-style. I had this delusion that sharing math class with him this year might actually lead to something, but instead, I just had to sit and watch him slobbering over her day after day. Still, there were too many potential pitfalls in creating a bogus boyfriend. What if we got caught? We'd had umpteen assemblies about bullying and cyberbullying. I'm pretty sure concocting a fantasy boyfriend would qualify. I can't remember exactly—wasn't there some news story, some girl, some state law . . . ?

But Tori and Eva don't listen, of course. They begin discussing strategy over my head, ignoring me completely—something they do more and more lately. Why is it that sometimes, the loneliest place in the world is sitting right in between my two so-called best friends?

"It'll never work," I say.

"It will," Eva insists. "But for this to be believable, it has to be someone real. We need someone who doesn't already have a profile."

"Yeah, but, like who?" Tori wrinkles her nose in confusion, unable to imagine a world where someone could have no online presence.

"There must be someone . . ." Eva doesn't seem at all deterred, so I try another tactic, pointing out that Cooper isn't my boyfriend and can date whomever he pleases. This only makes her sigh in frustration. "Noelle, you need to get over this shy thing and make a move already. Something he can't ignore. Just go jump his bones. I mean, we're not freshman, anymore."

I shake my head, looking away. Doesn't she get it? I've thought about it a hundred times. Well, not jumping his bones. But telling Cooper how I feel. But it's too much of a gamble. What if he shoots me down? What if he finds me repulsive? What if it turns our friendship into something all awkward? I just can't take the risk.

Tori eyes me critically. "Plus, you're ten zillion times cuter than she is. I mean, boobs aside, you have to give her that." But Tori is just being loyal. Annalise is the kind of girl who's hard to miss. She has curves to die for and traffic-stopping, reddish curly hair. She gets noticed without even trying. My looks are cute enough to get by on. Straight brown hair, large brown eyes like a trusty basset hound. Nothing special.

"Right."

Hearing the doubt in my voice, Tori insists it is true in the way she knows best. "Seriously. I mean, if I set up a pageant between you two, you'd totally win."

Reflexively, I make a face. "Don't you even!"

I don't want any part of Tori's pageant. Early in their friendship, she'd put herself and Eva in the same pageant, and Eva had received two fewer "likes." After that little episode, they practically didn't talk for a whole week. But we never mention *that*, either.

Eva stands up and slings an arm around me, her voice softer this time. "We're just going to chat with her. What's the harm? Besides, we're doing this for you, Noey. Because I just want you to be happy. Like me and Amos. With Annalise out of the way you totally have a chance with him. You guys could be so good together."

Her words warm me. I do want what Eva and Amos have. A real boyfriend, not just a hook up. Someone to hold hands with during basketball games. Send me flowers on Valentine's Day. Maybe even some top-secret, late-night sexts. There is a connection there, I know it. But how much longer will Annalise stay immune to Cooper's full court press?

Eva sees me shrug and relent, and before I know what's happened, she's shouting, "Brainstorm! I've got the perfect guy!" She races over to my bed, snatches up her rhinestone-clad iPhone where she'd left it, and begins scrolling back through her photos until she finds what she's looking for. "My second cousin, Declan. He lives way out in Worcester. He's cute, I guess, but a total dork. He's this homeschool freak, and his parents don't allow him to do anything online. They're like, off the grid. He does, like, chess and fencing and takes classes at the science museum. That's it."

She holds the screen up for me and Tori to see, and I have to admit, Declan's not heinous. He's decently tall, with really intense dark hair and eyes and is wearing a retro Disney World T-shirt. Tori gives Declan's picture her professional appraisal, then nods her approval. Eva smiles, grabbing the cord to sync her phone to my computer, and a minute later, the photo of the two of them sitting at a picnic table pops up on my screen.

"Where were you?" Tori asks, squinting at the background.

"Oh, our family reunion. At my grandma's house. Apparently, I've got, like, twenty second cousins," Eva says as she deftly crops herself out of the image. I have to admit, I'm impressed; all those hours on Instagram have given her some wicked editrix skills. She is typing madly while we watch, Tori in amusement, and me, fascinated into paralysis. When she is done, she spins around and points at her handiwork, triumph shining in her eyes.

"*Voilà!* Meet Annalise Bradley's dream guy."

CHAPTER 3

ANNALISE

Why hasn't my mom returned any of my texts?

Especially today, when she knows I'm counting on her? Isn't she the one always lecturing how she expects *me* to answer her messages promptly? The whole forty-minute bus ride home, I'm freaking out because I still haven't heard back. Where is she? Usually, she takes the night shifts, so she can be around when I'm home from school, but maybe some last-minute emergency called her in to the hospital?

Maeve had to talk me off a limb during lunch period, and has texted me twice from volleyball tryouts, asking if we got the tickets, and I still don't know what to tell her. I burst into the house, breathless from jogging up the driveway, where I find my mom, totally alive and unscathed, sitting at the kitchen table, chatting merrily away on the phone. Unbelievable. As soon as she sees me, she holds up her finger and gives me the universal "one sec" sign, which always means fifteen minutes at least, so I grab an apple from the fridge and hover over her, frantically waggling my eyebrows at her, hoping she'll cut her chat short.

Quickly, though, I can tell it's just not a call with a friend but somewhat serious; her end of the conversation mostly consists of "uh-huhs" and "okays" and jotting down random numbers on a scrap of paper.

The second she hangs up, I explode, "Mom! What happened? Didn't you get—"

But she is already sighing and slumping in her chair and talking over me. "You wouldn't believe the day I had. This woman in a honking Odyssey comes out of nowhere on Route 15. Totally took out the whole fender. Then we had to wait for the police to get there to file a report, then forty-five minutes for AAA to tow me a mile to the body shop. Two weeks, they need, can you believe it? So then I had to wait for Enterprise to drop off a rental. Which reeked of smoke, so I had to get another. Nightmare." She runs her fingers through her short brown hair in aggravation.

"Mom," I say, a twinge of dread prickling down my spine. "You did get the tickets, right? The concert?"

She gives me a pained look. "I know, I just saw all your texts, Lise. And your alert. I'm sorry, things were a little crazed. And my phone was dead."

"So that's a . . . no?"

Now my mom is giving me a death stare almost as bad as Eva's, her eyes like laser beams. I've gone too far. "Did you hear what I just said? How about, 'Are you okay, Mom? Were you hurt? I'm glad you survived a potentially fatal car crash without a scrape, Mom?' Really, Annalise. No, I didn't get the tickets. I just got in the house ten minutes ago. I'm sorry. Life happens."

Um. I am the Worst. Daughter. Ever. Because she is right. What if she'd been seriously injured? Or killed? Then what would happen? I know what: Elena and I would probably have to go off and live with Dad in North Carolina with his mistress-turned-new-wife Claire, or actually, just I would, since my sister's escaped life in Dansville a.k.a. Dullsville and is now a freshman at UMass Amherst. So it would just be me. Which would be a nightmare. But none of that is my mom's fault. She struggles mightily to keep things together, between being a single parent and her high-stress job as an X-ray tech. "Sorry, Mom. I just . . . I just . . ." I taper off, too upset to talk, my head reeling at this epic fail.

She heads over to her laptop, giving me a sympathetic smile. "Look, let's check online right now. I'm sure there's still something available. How quickly could they sell out?"

That quickly, Mom.

Five minutes later, a quick online search and phone call proves what I already know—they are gone gone gone. All of them.

"How can an arena that seats 10,000 people sell out in three hours?" My mom stubbornly argues with a customer service rep, while I click onto StubHub.com and find what I am looking for. "Mom, look! Front row tickets. Two of them!"

She comes over and looks over my shoulder at the screen. "Five hundred dollars?" Her voice is dark like thunder. "Ab-so-lute-ly not." I give her a pleading stare, although my babysitting stash won't come close and I know we don't have that kind of cash to spare. "Absolutely not!" she repeats, her voice rising an octave. "I'm sorry, that is just highway robbery. There's got to be another way."

"Like what?" I try to choke back a sob. I could ask if Dad would cough up the dough, but I know if I bring up his name, her face will get that sour look like she's just bitten into a lemon.

"I'm sorry, honey. Maybe you can see the band the next time they have a show. Or we can drive to a different venue?"

"That won't work," I shake my head, my chest tightening up. "This is their last stop. They just added it on. There is no other possible show . . ." I trail off, too upset to continue.

My mom puts her arm around me and gives me a squeeze. "Oh sweetie. I know you love this band right now, but let's get some perspective. Remember how much you used to like the Be Bop Brothers? And now you don't even play them anymore."

"That's not true!" I cry, breaking away. Actually, it was exactly true. Two years ago, I did have a total middle-school crush on Ramon, the guitarist for the Be Bop Brothers, and plastered the walls of my room with posters of his face. But this is different. For one thing, I've matured eons since then. Plus, Viggo Witts is an artist.

"Just . . . forget it." I grab my bag and rush up the stairs toward my room.

"Oh, and your father called," she yells up after me, using the term she now prefers for him. *Your. Father.*

"Great," I mutter, pulling my door open and slamming it shut behind me. Like I'd want to talk to him right now.

My mom doesn't get it. I've been dreaming of this moment forever. The chance to see Viggo Witts, live. In person. Breathe the same air. I couldn't believe my luck when they added this extra stop in Boston. Now, I'll never get to see him, let alone meet him. I collapse on my bed. I'd call Maeve, but she's probably in the middle of tryouts by now, and I don't want to blow her chances. Anyway, she's not really a true Knucklie like me; she's only tagging along because that's the kind of BFF she is. No, there's only one place where people will understand. I grab my laptop, click onto the Brass Knuckles fan page, and spill my sorrows onto the waiting wall.

KnuckLise99: devastated in dansville. lost out on tix for the upcoming show. can anyone help?

While I wait for a reply, I scroll back up and see all the other posts, mostly other Boston peeps bragging about what awesome tickets they scored, comparing seat locations and planning to meet up at intermission or find a way to get backstage access. I am consumed with jealousy. A bunch of the regulars—Juniper77,

DaisyFlour84—ping me back "no, sorry, that's too bad, wish I could help" but then suddenly, someone I don't recognize—someone new—lobs in a comment.

DecOlan: sorry, that sucks.
DecOlan: i didn't get tix either.
DecOlan: so what happened?

I hesitate for a second, then type a reply.

KnuckLise99: my mom was supposed to get them.
KnuckLise99: got in a fender bender instead.
KnuckLise99: now it's all sold out!
DecOlan: that's the worst. you can't be mad at her
DecOlan: but you can't help but be pissed.
KnuckLise99: exactly.
DecOlan: man, they are the best. i would eat nails to see them play live.
KnuckLise99: i know!!!! i've been #1 fan 4ever.
DecOlan: me too.

Weird he's never shown up on the site before, if he's such a big fan. Every other Knucklie in the universe has found their way here.

DecOlan: what's your fav song?
KnuckLise99: besides *Identity Crisis*? probably *Failing, Falling.*
DecOlan: mine too!
KnuckLise99: really?
DecOlan: yeah, genius right?
KnuckLise99: it's obviously his most meaningful work.
DecOlan: exactly.

KnuckLise99: the lyrics can be taken on so many different levels.

DecOlan: yes!!! i was just going to say that.

It was so cool to connect with another fan who got it, really got it. Most of the other posters on the fan site were girls who spent their time salivating over Viggo's perfect abs or cheekbones, but to be honest, few were guys, well, unless they were the types of guys who also salivated over his perfect abs and cheekbones. None of them ever got into analyzing the lyrics like this. While we chat about the meaning behind the words, I click over to his full profile to check him out. His full name is Declan O'Keefe, and he lives way out in Worcester, about an hour and a half west of the city. He's even posted a picture of himself (cute!) sitting alone on a picnic bench.

Suddenly, a personal InstaMessage from Declan pops up on my screen. I click to accept.

DecOlan: shhh. kinda sketch, but how about crashing the show without tix? :)

KnuckLise99: i'm in. how?

DecOlan: meet in the parking lot and listen from outside?

KnuckLise99: brilliant! just one problem.

DecOlan: ??

KnuckLise99: it's an enclosed arena.

DecOlan: d'oh! Ok . . . bribe the ushers to let us in?

KnuckLise99: wait wait! i know.

KnuckLise99: say we're covering it for the school paper and get press passes!!

DecOlan: no can do :(

KnuckLise99: ??

DecOlan: i don't go to skul.

I realize his profile page didn't list a school. What's up with that? My Stranger Danger alert gets triggered. Who is this guy, anyway? He looks my age, but you never know . . .

KnuckLise99: what are you, like, 50?
DecOlan: ha. 16. homeschooled.
KnuckLise99: cool. i guess. or is it?
DecOlan: Beats flipping burgers at Mickey D's.
KnuckLise99: don't you miss being around other kids? friends?
DecOlan: yeah, i need to get me some of those.
DecOlan: interested?

I chuckle out loud, amused. I don't know if he's serious or joking, but I'm flattered. And, what's the harm?

KnuckLise99: lol. sure why not?
DecOlan: because most people think we're unsocialized freaks.
KnuckLise99: r u?
DecOlan: dunno. test me.
KnuckLise99: ok. favorite book?
KnuckLise99: movie?
KnuckLise99: tv show?

And here's where it gets weird. It's crazy how much we have in common! Not just liking Brass Knuckles, but also our all-time favorite book (*The Great Gatsby*) and movie (*Clueless*), and even little things, like hating artichokes but loving asparagus, which we agree is downright eerie. I finally ask why he hasn't been on the fan page before, and he tells me that his parents have been really strict about letting him use social media, and have only just given in, now that he finally turned sixteen ("insane, right?"). I hear my mom calling me down to dinner, and even though I'm still mad at her, I'm also suddenly ravenous since I barely picked at my lunch.

KnuckLise99: mom calling. gtg.
DecOlan: ok. maybe we can talk later?
KnuckLise99: sure.
DecOlan: later, gator.

I head downstairs, for some reason unable to stop smiling. Missing the concert still completely blows, but I take some small comfort that in this whole sucktastic universe, at least I am not alone.

CHAPTER 4

NOELLE

I know nothing about being a guy.

That much is clear.

Eva, of course, had no problem posing as Declan. Her fingers flying over the keyboard, she chatted forever with Annalise about this and that. Music and books and whatnot, parroting back Annalise's likes without her suspecting a thing, Tori and me watching in awe over her shoulder the whole time.

The two of them thought it was soooo hilarious. How Annalise lapped it all up—that she and "Declan" just "happened" to share the same favorite song, the same books, even the same food likes and dislikes, all lifted right from her old posts.

But then they broke for dinner and Eva went home, dumping the whole crazy project in my lap, saying I should take over since she and Tori were going to be much too busy with after-school play rehearsals. Now, I have no clue how to pick up where she left off. What, exactly, do guys say to girls they're trying to hit on, online? I sit staring at the keyboard, trying to figure out where to begin. How a guy—our guy, our made up, fictional guy, Declan O'Keefe, who is a real person but not exactly—would sweet talk a girl.

Hey.
Wassup?
Yo.

That's how most guys at my school talk, as if monosyllabic grunts pass for scintillating conversation. *Except for Cooper,* my inner voice pipes in. He's the only guy I know who's easy to talk to. Then again, he's like that with everyone. If Cooper had a motto, it would be: *I never met a man I didn't like.* And he sure doesn't have any trouble yakking away to Annalise in math every day.

The trouble is I'm a complete novice in the guy department. Eva's been dating Amos forever, and Tori's had guys pursuing her since she was in vitro. I'm the only one who's had practically no interaction with the male species, thanks to my dumb reputation as a brain. Just my crush on Cooper, dating back to when our parents enrolled us in Little Quackers Preschool down in our church basement when we were three. Problem is, in his eyes, I haven't matured any since then. He still treats me like I'm his sandbox buddy, just minus the sand.

"Charm her, tell her she's hot, whatever you have to do," Eva had instructed me as she flounced her way out the door, probably seeing the look of panic on my face. "This is for you, Noelle," she pointedly reminded me. "For you and Cooper, right?" So now, like always, I'm doing what she told me to. After dinner with my parents, I escape back to my room and log in again as "Declan." I send a message saying, you there? to Annalise, then sit, staring at the screen, waiting nervously to see if she will respond. Within seconds, she does. Before I can come up with something else to say, she has a question for me.

KnuckLise99: forgot to ask before—why didn't *you* get tickets?

Good question, right? If I'm such a Knucklie, why *didn't* I get tickets? I grope around for a reason that sounds legit. Money issues? Scheduling conflict? Strict parents?

DecOlan: i'm grounded.
DecOlan: no phone.
DecOlan: no outings.
DecOlan: computer for "educational purposes" only. <<sly grin>>

I smile, pleased that I landed on this response, which serves two purposes. This way, if Annalise wants to meet, or get my number to text me, I have a built-in excuse. No cell, no going out for the time being.

KnuckLise99: aw. what for?

For what? Another good question. I break into a sweat. Lying in real time is harder than it looks. What do guys our age get grounded for, anyway? Downloading porn, most likely. But I don't want her thinking "Declan" is some creepy perv. Smoking? No way, I'm pretty sure Annalise wouldn't go for a guy with stinky ashtray breath. Getting busted for drinking? I decide to play coy until I can think of a convincing misdeed.

DecOlan: i'd tell you . . .
DecOlan: but first I'd have to know you better ;)

I hit return and hold my breath. Too bold? Too obvious? There's a pause, while I wait for Annalise to reply. I wonder what she's thinking. Then, she finally types a response:

KnuckLise99: there's not much to know.

DecOlan: i doubt that.

KnuckLise99: trust me.

DecOlan: ok. well then . . . what's your sign?

KnuckLise99: gemini.

KnuckLise99: why? do you believe in astrology?

DecOlan: nope.

DecOlan: those were my dad's first words to my mom. true story.

KnuckLise99: <<shocked>> hard to believe that actually worked.

DecOlan: well i'm here aren't i?

KnuckLise99: theoretically.

DecOlan: lol.

KnuckLise99: still, a little dated, as pick up lines go . . .

DecOlan: i'd call it, timeless.

DecOlan: and who says i'm trying to pick you up? <<innocent expression>>

KnuckLise99: riiiiight.

KnuckLise99: so does that line work on all the girls?

DecOlan: dunno. first time at bat.

KnuckLise99: <<raises skeptical eyebrow>>

DecOlan: how am i doing so far?

KnuckLise99: honestly, pretty mediocre. C-

DecOlan: <<crushed>>

KnuckLise99: ok maybe a C+. <<grudgingly>> i grade on a curve.

DecOlan: ooof. tough critic. here's a better question.

KnuckLise99: shoot.

DecOlan: is your relationship status really single?

KnuckLise99: yes.

DecOlan: i find that hard to believe.

KnuckLise99: why?

DecOlan: come on. <<blushing>> don't make me say it.

Even from a digital distance, I can tell Annalise is smiling. She must be. What girl wouldn't be eating this up? I know I would. Instead, she abruptly changes the subject.

KnuckLise99: then don't.
KnuckLise99: my turn.
KnuckLise99: how come *your* status is single?
DecOlan: tough to meet cute chicks when you're homeschooled and dad's your wingman.
KnuckLise99: so why homeschooled? you're not part of some crazy religious cult, trapped in your basement?
DecOlan: ha ha, no.
KnuckLise99: child star?
DecOlan: i wish.
KnuckLise99: not dying of some horrible terminal illness before your time?
DecOlan: nothing that dramatic. my dad can't stand govt skul rules.
DecOlan: crazy union teaching to the test.
DecOlan: yadda yadda.
KnuckLise99: so what do you do all day?

The question catches me off guard. What *do* homeschooled kids do all day? How should I know? I just start making it up, based on the little Eva had told me about Declan and my imagination.

DecOlan: ya know. worksheets all morning. then freedom the rest of the day. i read. sketch. play online chess. there's meetups, sometimes. at museums and stuff. with other families.

DecOlan: wow. typing that out makes me realize how completely lame my life is.

KnuckLise99: no. it just sounds pretty . . . solitary.

DecOlan: yeah. it's not a bunch of pep rallies and prom committees.

KnuckLise99: ha! so not my life.

DecOlan: at least you're around actual humans all day long.

KnuckLise99: assuming the kids at my school are human.

KnuckLise99: plus, ever heard the expression alone in a crowd?

That comment throws me. I pause, startled to hear my earlier thoughts echoed back at me. I know I feel that way around Tori and Eva, but does she really feel that way, too? I mean, true, she's not on the pep squad, but Annalise is not some total outcast. She has friends. Well, a friend. Isn't she always with that tall, sarcastic girl with the glasses, what's her name, Mauve? Maeve. Then again, we had been pretty harsh after the Amos incident and most of the girls in our grade had taken our side. I wonder if she is speaking the truth. Or at least, her truth.

I shake my head, trying to shoo away sympathy like a pesky housefly that won't leave me alone. I know what Eva would say. She asked for it, didn't she? With what she did? And she sure doesn't seem to mind all the male attention she gets as a result. Including Cooper.

DecOlan: come on. you don't strike me as the loner type.

DecOlan: you sure don't look like a girl who sits home Saturday night.

There. What girl doesn't want to hear that a guy thinks she's hot? Apparently, Annalise. Because she shoots back a terse reply.

KnuckLise99: where do you get that?

Whoa. Red alert. Somehow, I have majorly offended her. This conversation is headed in the entirely wrong direction.

DecOlan: i just meant—
KnuckLise99: cuz, you don't really know me.
KnuckLise99: you don't know anything about me.

What happened? I thought this was going so well. If I screw this up, Eva and Tori are going to think I am pathetic. And Cooper is going to slip away. My fingers fly back to the keyboard, but I am too late.

KnuckLise99: this was a mistake.
DecOlan: wait.
KnuckLise99: i gotta go.
DecOlan: no.
DecOlan: please.
DecOlan: i'm—

Before I can type another word, I see her user name has gone gray. She is gone.

DecOlan: —sorry.

CHAPTER 5

ANNALISE

How. Dare. He.

This Declan O'Keefe, making all sorts of assumptions about me, based on what? *You don't look like a girl who sits home Saturday night.* It's obviously code for, you look like a slut. Right? Except, where was he getting that from? I scroll back through our convo, trying to see if I'd written anything to give that impression. Did I miss something? Why did I start spilling my guts to some random guy I don't even know? I should have known better.

Obviously, Declan had wasted no time checking out my profile photo. And all right, sure, I'd done the same to him, but I still can't help but feel a little . . . what? Offended? Invaded? Anyway, the image I'd uploaded was a carefully chosen, casual head shot, nothing racy at all. I enlarge it and study my own face, trying to figure out what Declan had seen. Curly reddish-brown hair. Petite nose. Plump lips. Does something about me give off some slutty vibe? Some Scarlet A, just like in that god-awful boring Hawthorne book—except the "A" stands for Annalise instead of adulteress? Maybe that's why Amos targeted me in the first place.

Well, forget it. This Declan is obviously just like every other guy on the planet. Like my own father, even. Not to be trusted, like my mom is always saying, and—happy now, Mother?—turned out to be right. I had been feeling a smidgeon of guilt for never calling my dad back, but why bother? He has a new family now, a new city, a new life. Spending time this summer with him, my stepmonster, and the toddler twins, a fifth wheel to his perfect new family, made all that perfectly clear. So instead of calling him back, I turn to the only thing that always makes me feel better. I put on my favorite Brass Knuckles playlist, pop my earbuds in my ears so my mom won't complain the music is too loud, and think about Viggo Witts, who would never let me down.

I troll online for anything new on the band and something pops up: a video interview posted on Buzznewz, where Viggo talks in his adorable accent about how the world is full of *bling-bling fakety-fakers*, and how he came up with the idea for his soon-to-be released song "Inner Beauty" after his D-list wannabe ex-girlfriend, Skye, the Abercrombie model, dragged him to New York's Fashion Week. All the other fangirls on the Brass Knuckles feed had been threatened by her freakish beauty, but I never was. It was so obvious that their two-week fling was just a dumb publicity stunt.

When the clip ends, a pop-up ad teasing the latest issue of *Seventeen* online catches my eye: HATE YOUR BODY? LEARN TO LOVE IT!!! I click, and there is the obligatory quiz, which I quickly scan:

You are invited to a pool party. You:
a. Decline.
b. Show up in a tankini.
c. Show up in a bikini.
d. Show up in a one-piece bathing suit—covered by a burka.

Even more useless is the fashion spread, where all the girls have body issues, like a tiny bit of muffin top, or thick ankles, or a flat chest, all one . . . two . . . three . . . presto! fixed with a simple fashion tip (Spanx! gladiator sandals! a Miracle Bra!) from the editors (click *here* to purchase!) that magically cure their perceived flaws. None of which would work on my boob problem.

When I'd begged my mom for a reduction last year, she had sighed and told me that those were only for teens who were grotesquely huge, and whose backs ached all the time, and could interfere with breastfeeding (ick) a baby someday—which as far as I was concerned was a total bonus. You're just on the curvy side, she'd told me. Consider yourself lucky. *Lucky??* She'd told me we could talk about it in another year or two, once I'd definitely stopped growing. *Hold on, I might be still growing??* What she didn't say was that the procedure was crazy expensive and probably wasn't covered by health insurance. I'd started a secret boob reduction kitty, but so far, my stash consisted of about $387 of birthday checks from my dad, allowance, and babysitting money, which wouldn't even cover the cost of the anesthesia.

My mom doesn't seem to get that my boobs have ruined my life. How their surprise appearance in seventh grade tanked my spot on the Flip It! competitive gymnastics team, which I'd only been doing since I was five, sure that I'd grow up to be the next Aly Raisman and win the gold for the US of A. It was obvious, when I saw the lineup of petite flat-chested girls that made the team, that the problem wasn't my technique or my dedication or my flexibility, it was obviously my, ahem, newfound physique.

If only I had a boyish bod like Elena or Maeve, maybe I would have had a shot at the medal by now. But when my body changed, so did my chance of athletic glory. There was no way I'd excel at any other sport, either: forget track, crew, or volleyball. All I can see are the dreams my stupid big boobs have crushed. Imagine the *Seventeen* editors trying to come up with a quiz designed for girls like me:

You have grotesquely huge boobs. Which super-cool career will you choose?

    a.   Hooters Girl (gross)

    b.   Victoria Secret model (grosser)

    c.   Stripper at the Golden Banana (grossest)

    d.   La Leche League lactation leader (ewwww)

You'd think boobs would at least give you an edge with getting a real live boyfriend, but all they've gotten me are snickers and stares and rude comments from total jerk-offs. Like the time in eighth grade when Tyler Walters asked me if sleeping on my stomach was like being on a seesaw all night. Ha ha. Or guys like Cooper, with one item on their agendas. Thank god beach season was over and it was fall, a season where you could safely layer on the slouchy sweaters and hoodies without looking like a freak.

My phone pings, interrupting my thoughts. It is Maeve, finally checking in after tryouts.

MaeveRose: so?? tix??

KnuckLise99: nope. mom decided to crash car instead.

MaeveRose: !!!!!???

KnuckLise99: long story. drama.

MaeveRose: seriously no tix? r u ok?

KnuckLise99: pretty much suicidal.

MaeveRose: don't u freakin dare leave me all alone at dullsville high!

KnuckLise99: jk. how were tryouts?

MaeveRose: good i think. list up tomorrow.

KnuckLise99: you'll so make it.

MaeveRose: fingers crossed! gtg. so tired . . . mounds of homework. need to crash.

KnuckLise99: me too. nite.

MaeveRose: nite.

After I tell my mom I'm going to sleep, I get in bed and close my eyes. I settle in with my music, thinking how Viggo obviously wants more than something superficial with a girl like Skye, and really, he's only two years older than me, and if only I could find a way to get to that concert and lock eyes with him, I just know we'd connect for real. But even Viggo Witts's silken voice has a hard time easing me off to sleep tonight, with the drumbeat of Declan's last words pounding through my mind.

CHAPTER 6
NOELLE

All morning, I've tried not to panic about messing things up with Annalise. What if Eva asks me in math class how last night's conversation went? What if she logs on after school and sees for herself? My only hope is to get things back on track—before she gets a clue. But how?

Luckily, the perfect person to ask races into World History. Tori. The queen of placating the bruised egos and hurt feelings she's left in her wake. She's forever telling us about the latest pageant kerfuffle, like the contestant who accused the winner of cheating by getting her whole Pom Squad to "like" her photo in exchange for a shot at being co-captain.

She exhales loudly and slides into her seat like it's home plate, seconds before the final bell rings. Her perfectly highlighted locks are limp from sweat, and her clothes look like they were crumpled up in a locker for the last hour. Which they probably were. Even a wreck, with her long honey-blond hair and longer spray-tanned legs, most girls I know would still take looking like Tori D'Fillipo on P.E. day.

"Gym?" I murmur sympathetically, as half the guys in the room swivel their heads to check her out.

"Deitrich made us run, like, a hundred laps around in the rain," she says, panting slightly. "It was brutal." It's only the second week of school, and Tori still hasn't gotten over the indignity of getting stuck in first-period gym. To her, it's a disruption in the natural order of things, like blush before foundation. "She wouldn't even let us stop to get a drink of water. I mean, isn't that like, a human rights violation, or something?"

I'm guessing she means waterboarding, but I just nod my head. At least the scheduling gods blessed me with a late-day gym class.

"I can't stand her. Seriously. That stupid whistle. Like what are we, dogs? And those shorts she wears. And her untouched roots." She swivels her head, looking around the room for our absent history teacher. "Where's Gewirtz?"

I shrug and tell her she must be late.

Tori slumps, now annoyed she made the effort to arrive on time.

"Plus, I can't look a mess. Auditions are after school today!" She eyes me curiously. "Sure you're not trying out?"

I shake my head vehemently. "No way." Performing in *High School Musical*, getting up on stage, even for a part in the chorus, sounds like *my* idea of a war crime. Pure torture. Tori shrugs and pulls out a compact, trying to fix her smudged eyeliner, and asks to see my homework. I pull it out and silently pass it over to her.

"So, do you think your mom might have some new product soon?" she says as her eyes quickly scan my work, double-checking her own answers.

I nod and tell her I think so, knowing next season's product line should be arriving any day, and my mom always brings home some extra samples for me and my friends.

"Can you tell her I could really use some lotion? The fall air is so drying. Actually, there's something else I wanted to ask her. Eva and I came up with it last night."

This is news. I feel a sudden stab of insecurity that they'd been chatting without me while I'd been busy romancing Annalise. How often do their late-night discussions exclude me?

"Do you think her company would consider sponsoring my pageant?" Tori asks, her blue eyes lighting up with excitement. "They could, like, offer samples as prizes, and I could do some product placement, like, suggest their stuff to the losers, that sort of thing?"

It sounds like the worst idea I've ever heard, pushing cosmetics on dejected beauty pageant losers, but what do I know? Maybe it's pure evil genius.

"I'll ask," I say, feeling slightly off-put, but mostly relieved the topic of conversation wasn't me and all my shortcomings. Sometimes, I wonder whether Tori would still be my friend if my mom sold medical devices instead of makeup. Or if I weren't helping her from failing history.

"Great!" She rewards me with a toothy beam. "She's the best." Her phone buzzes. "Hold on," she says, pulling it from her pocket and checking the screen. "Ugh," she rolls her eyes. "These needy pageant girls are driving me nuts with their whining." She doesn't reply, shoving her phone back into her skin-tight white jean skirt. If Tori had a motto, it would be: *if you can't stand the heat, get out of the kitchen.* "Sometimes, I just want to tell them, 'You lost. Get over it.' You know?"

Then why do it? I want to ask, but just nod instead.

"Oh! So how's the you-know-what going?" Her voice is loud, too loud, but luckily our teacher is still MIA and the room has grown as raucous as the monkey house at the Franklin Park Zoo.

I confess that things are not going well. I'm guessing Tori won't take my screw up personally, since this crazy project wasn't her baby, but Eva's.

She looks surprised. "Already? What happened?"

I hesitate. "Don't tell Eva, until I fix it, okay?"

"Oooh, intrigue." She arches a dutifully waxed eyebrow and leans in. "I won't say a word, I promise."

I wonder if I'm about to make a big mistake. Can I trust her to keep my secret? Especially since she's really more Eva's friend than mine. After the two of them bonded last fall at play rehearsals, Eva eagerly adopted Tori into our clique, never thinking to ask if I wanted to expand our cozy twosome.

Tori insists I spill it, so I tell her in detail how I blew my first online encounter with Annalise, trying to flatter her and instead somehow insulting her.

She shakes her head in disappointment. "Not good. You better win her back. Pronto."

I ask how and she nods, Yoda-like, considering her words. "You know what always works, for hurt feelings?" she finally says. "You should try a sorry kitty."

Whatever I had been expecting her to say, this wasn't it.

"A sorry—what?"

She pulls out her phone again and scrolls through her images. Eventually, she finds what she is looking for and shows me the picture on her screen. A small white kitten sits adorably tangled in a basket of unraveled yarn twisted like a multicolored bowl of spaghetti. The kitten looks apologetically at the camera, as if it wishes it could mew something. And in fact, the caption reads "I'm Sorry."

I shake my head, pretty sure I'm not *that* desperate. Besides, what if Annalise is a dog person? I'm looking for the grand gesture, the thing that will win her back, convince her she was wrong about me. The Declan me, that is.

"Try it," she insists, tapping out a message, sending it to me, then quickly jamming her phone back into her bag as our history teacher, Ms. Gewirtz, finally bursts into the room, breathless and holding a stack of pop quizzes fresh from the copier, eliciting a collective class groan. "Never underestimate the power of a sorry kitty."

CHAPTER 7

ANNALISE

At lunch today, I finally debrief Maeve on the complete fiasco of how my mom didn't get us the concert tickets. The car crash. The dead phone. The StubHub ripoff pricing structure.

"Mon Dieu!" she says, lapsing into Conversational French, her last class before lunch. Madame LeFouge requires all her students to speak French exclusively all period long, and sometimes the habit sticks. "Quel dommage!"

"English, por favor," I have to remind her. "Yo no hablo French."

"Sorry, sorry." She stabs her french fries with a fork and pops one in her mouth.

"So do you want to come over today after school?" I ask, sipping my chemical-laden no-cal sports drink, which I've grown addicted to now that our school bans sugary sodas. "Maybe we can search craigslist for cheap tickets?"

"Love to but . . . no can do," she says, her face breaking into a wide grin. "Practice starts today!"

"What? Did you—"

Her face beams as she nods, relishing the surprised look on my face. "Yup. Made the team!"

"That's awesome!" I say, giving her a hug. "Way to bury the lede." I can't believe she let me go on and on about the concert ticket debacle with news this huge.

She mimes a pretend spike over an imaginary net. "I totally rocked the tryouts! Are you in awe of my awesomeness?"

"I am," I say, knowing how hard it is for a sophomore to break onto a team, even though Coach Deitrich had practically begged her to try out after seeing Maeve's volleyball skills in gym class last year. "I'm not worthy."

I jokingly bow down to her, although part of me feels a sinking sensation. Team sports mean practice every day after school. When will I see her now? It's bad enough that all winter, her family goes skiing every weekend up in New Hampshire, leaving me solo when all the girls in our class are having sleepovers or going skating at the Ice Palace. And ever since she was ten, Maeve has gone off to some sleep-away camp in Maine, leaving me stuck on my own all summer. And now, she's not even going to be free to hang out after school, like, ever? It's hard relying on only one best friend, especially when she doesn't have all that much free time for you. It's exponentially worse when everyone seems to think that talking to you will somehow rub your pariah fumes onto them.

To be honest, this year hasn't been so bad so far. The summer break seems to have reset most people's memories of last year's rumors. Maya Gomez asked me to sign her petition to run for student government. Even Tess McDonohue, one of Eva's crew, whose locker is next to mine, asked to borrow a pen during the first week of school, thanking me without a single trace of snottiness in her tone.

I think again of Declan and his comment on friends: *yeah, i need to get me some of those. interested?* For some reason, I hadn't mentioned Declan to Maeve, even though part of me is curious to know what she'd think. That he was an online creep I was right to defriend? Or, more likely, that he'd been trying to compliment me, and I flipped out like a psycho. But I'm embarrassed to admit to Maeve that I even care. Which I don't. It was just some random guy I chatted with on some random night. Besides, what's the difference? I'll probably never hear from him again.

I'm not sure I even want to.

Then after school, he pings me: *hey, are you still mad?*

Delete. Next. Easy to ignore.

And again, the next day. *I didn't mean to piss you off.* But this time, his words come attached to a photo of this adorable white kitty tangled in a basket of yarn, with her paws begging for forgiveness, and the caption "I'm Sorry."

My fingers pause. Really? A sorry kitty? On what planet did he think *that* would work? Guys can be so clueless about females. Delete. Then, the next day, he pings me again, a long message with a small file attached. Instead of trashing it right away, I read what he says. Twice.

DecOlan: look. i'll try one more time and then leave you alone forever. <<deep breath>> i totally take back what i said—you look like you spend all your weekend nights home alone. you're most likely a shut-in. and a hoarder. with a huge goiter. and really gnarly chin hairs. there. feel better?

I have to laugh. Like, true, laugh out loud laugh. Something about his sense of humor gets to me. Maybe I was too harsh. Anyway, Maeve is off at practice, so who else do I have to talk to? I am this close to writing him back, but before I can think what to reply, he is typing again.

DecOlan: now, before you delete this, make sure you check out the file.

DecOlan: i got it just for you.

Just for me? Curious, I go ahead and click on it.

Up pops an audio file titled "Inner Beauty," and when I push play, my ears almost fall off my head. It's Viggo Witts, singing a song I've never heard before in my life, which I didn't think was possible. From the lyrics and the file name, though, I recognize instantly what it must be: the unreleased single from their upcoming album! The one he was talking about in that video clip. But how did Declan get this? Ignoring the teensy detail that I'm still supposedly mad and never talking to him again, my fingers sputter over the keyboard.

KnuckLise99: is this their new song?
DecOlan: oh, ho ho. so now you're speaking to me?
KnuckLise99: how did you get this??
DecOlan: i have my sources.
KnuckLise99: COME ON! dying here.
DecOlan: ok. yes, it's their new release.
DecOlan: some guy in london bootlegged their recording session.
KnuckLise99: how'd you get it?
DecOlan: sent him $5 bucks on paypal.
KnuckLise99: seriously?
DecOlan: i don't joke about cross-atlantic financial transactions.
KnuckLise99: ha ha. you rock!
DecOlan: soooo, does this mean i'm forgiven?
DecOlan: If not, this message will self-destruct in 5 . . . 4 . . . 3 . . .

How can you stay mad at someone who's just given you a bootlegged copy of the new Brass Knuckles song before it's even been released? You just can't, that's how.

KnuckLise99: you are totally forgiven! <<kneels down at feet>> i'm sorry i tore your head off.

DecOlan: no, it's all on me. <<smiley face>> i should never have paid you a compliment. what was i thinking?

Pause. He is right. I feel like such a fool for overreacting like that. Over a compliment from a guy. Why hadn't I told Maeve? She would have given me perspective.

KnuckLise99: what can I say? i've got issues.
DecOlan: there's gotta be a course for that. compliment taking 101.
KnuckLise99: i'm messed up.
DecOlan: who isn't?
KnuckLise99: lets just say i've been burned before. by the male species.
DecOlan: men are dogs. or so i've heard.
DecOlan: so what happened?

Pause. I want to tell him why I'm such a nut case, about my dad, about Amos. I want to tell him everything, want to finally tell someone impartial, who would believe my side of the story, unlike most of my classmates, who mostly believed *them*. Eva. And Amos. But I can't. It all still hurts too much. So I fall back on the words he'd used on me.

KnuckLise99: i'd tell you . . . but first I'd have to know you better ;)
DecOlan: touché, m'lady. touché.

I can't go there with Declan. Not yet. Maybe not ever.

CHAPTER 8
NOELLE

It's funny how the one thing you dread doing at first can sometimes turn into something you can't wait to do over and over again. Like the time I was nine, and terrified to cannonball off the high diving board at the town pool for the very first time. After I took that first dizzying leap, you couldn't drag me away the rest of the summer. So even though I could never, ever confess this to Eva and Tori, talking to Annalise every night, which once filled me with dread, has now somehow become the highlight of my day.

At school, I'll hear something funny or weird or odd, and instead of wanting to tell Eva, I find myself filing it away to tell Annalise later that night. We talk way late, even until 1 A.M., typing away in the dark after my parents have gone to sleep. There's literally nothing we don't discuss: Knucklie news, of course, but everything else: presidential politics, our crazy parents, the It Gets Better campaign, which is more addictive, Candy Crush or Words With Friends, where we were the day of the Boston Marathon bombings, whether teachers should be armed with semis, how the Baby Boomers have totally screwed up the planet, Disney versus Universal, whether to stockpile bitcoins, the possibility of an afterlife, and how we wouldn't be caught dead twerking.

Sometimes, it gets confusing, like this one time we were playing "Marry Bang Kill" and I forgot for a half-second that I'm supposed to be a guy, and almost came up with the completely wrong list of celebrities, but so far, she hasn't caught on. And it's hard not to feel like a double agent, trying to reconcile two people in my life—the Annalise I'm supposed to hate by day, and the Annalise I can't wait to talk to online each night. At times, my head feels like it's going to explode.

Still, I thought I'd completely nailed impersonating Declan, studying up on Brass Knuckles trivia, so Annalise wouldn't catch me unawares of some arcane band factoid. That's how I stumbled upon a tip on some UK message board for scoring that advance version of "Inner Beauty," which was a bit trickier and costlier than I let on.

And then I slipped up. Big time. It started when we were talking about some reality TV star and her bafflingly dumb decision to dry hump her microphone onstage during the Golden Globes.

KnuckLise99: what was she thinking?
DecOlan: beats me.
KnuckLise99: people are so random.
DecOlan: unfathomable.
KnuckLise99: mindboggling.
DecOlan: and yet we all share 99.99999% of the same genes.
KnuckLise99: i'd rather share DNA with an ape than that mutant starlet.
DecOlan: lol.
KnuckLise99: and yet . . .
DecOlan: and yet?
KnuckLise99: someone said the other day that deep down, we're all the same.
KnuckLise99: we may look different.

KnuckLise99: but we all have the same wants, desires, needs.

I carefully consider that notion. I think of the people I know: my outgoing mom, the cosmetics executive who loves schmoozing people, and my introverted dad, a financial analyst who'd rather deal with numbers than human beings. I think of Eva, who invites attention, auditioning for and winning the lead in the school play, and me, who shuns it. I think of Cooper, who says every thought passing through his head, while I over-think everything I say.

DecOlan: i disagree.
DecOlan: completely.
DecOlan: have you taken a look at humankind? the crazy variation?
DecOlan: chatters and lurkers.
DecOlan: optimists and pessimists.
DecOlan: exhibitionists and prudes.
KnuckLise99: but isn't it true we all want the same thing?
DecOlan: like what?
KnuckLise99: love, respect, security.
DecOlan: then how come we go about getting it in completely different ways?

Further debate is cut off by a knock at my door. I quickly write her a "be right back" and close the browser window.

"Noelle?" It's my dad. "You going to bed anytime tonight?"

Soon, I tell him.

"What were you doing? Talking to Eva?" He frowns, eyeing the blank computer screen, and I mind read what he is thinking. My parents don't particularly like Eva. They say she "pressures me into making bad choices." And that's just based on the things they *know* about, not all the things they don't—the time we jumped off Nook's Bridge and my toenail caught on a rock and got ripped clean off. The night we borrowed an unlocked dinghy and went out to the spit to drink wine coolers and almost capsized. I can't say I entirely disagree with them.

"No, Tori," I say, knowing his opinion on Tori is more neutral, still unformed.

His tie is loose and there are tired shadows under his eyes.

I'm dying to get back to my discussion with Annalise, but I feel compelled to ask, "Is everything okay?"

He smiles, and the wrinkles around his eyes grow crinkly, to go with the newish flecks of grey in his dark sideburns. "Just a rough day at work." I know what he means. He's looked this way ever since he got this new boss last winter. I spent a few days in his office this summer, and I couldn't believe how rude he was—screaming over any screw up, no matter whose fault it was. He's always calling my dad at night, even over the weekends. You can hear the shouting reverberating through the tiny cell phone speaker.

I wish he would just tell this evil overlord to suck it. Tess McDonohue told me she's quitting her job at Au Bon Pain because her assistant manager is a petty, power-drunk tyrant who docks her pay every time she gets an order wrong—but forgives every screw up of her skanky coworker, SaraBeth.

"Can't you just quit?" I ask him, although I think I already know the answer.

He smiles ruefully. "Just like that, huh?"

"Why not?" I reply boldly. "No one can make you feel inferior without your consent. Know whose motto that was?"

He smiles and tousles my hair like he did when I was eight. "Eleanor Roosevelt. When did you get so smart?" But then he sighs. "When you're an adult . . . it's not so simple."

"Maybe it should be."

"Maybe." He stands up and stretches his spine. "But it'll be fine. I'll be fine. Just need a good night's sleep. You, too. Not too late, okay?"

"Okay."

"Love you."

When he leaves, I check to see if Annalise is still there. She picks right back up where we left off, as if she too has been eagerly waiting to continue.

KnuckLise99: then what makes us so different?

KnuckLise99: nature or nurture?

DecOlan: false question.

DecOlan: it's both. little of each.

KnuckLise99: ok. name one moment that's defined you. made you you?

I don't even have to think hard, my hands are already typing away.

DecOlan: easy. choking at my 6th grade concert.

KnuckLise99: choking?

KnuckLise99: Like Heimlich choking?

DecOlan: no, like freezing.

DecOlan: messing up.

Mrs. Byrd, our music teacher, assigned us all a singing part during our rendition of "Twelve Days of Christmas." Me and Tamara Winger were supposed to sing together, which was fine in rehearsals, because she was really loud so I could just chime in softly along with her. But then she ended up with strep that December morning and I had to sing the line by myself. When it came time to sing *fiiiiive gol-den rings*, I just froze. Completely froze. Every time the verse came around to me, it was like I had instant laryngitis.

Afterwards, some of the boys in the class started this dumb joke called Noelling, where they'd gape for air like a goldfish on dry land. Until Eva came to my rescue. She hauled off and smacked their ringleader, Tyler Walters, just really smacked him across the face with the side of her hand, leaving a red mark. After that, no one said another word about it, and I made sure I never got up on a stage again. And for the rest of middle school and beyond, I always knew that Eva had my back.

I feel a familiar twinge of guilt over this late-night bonding with her sworn nemesis. Then the words pop up on my screen:

KnuckLise99: wait. what do you mean 6th grade?

I stare at them, realizing my mistake. Ack! I panic at this amateurish flub. I'm supposed to be homeschooled. How could I forget? I scramble to issue a retraction.

DecOlan: my bad.
DecOlan: meant, when I was 6. last year I was in school. first grade holiday concert.
DecOlan: left me with a serious case of stage fright.

Have I covered myself? I pray Annalise buys it. Quickly, I turn the tables on her.

DecOlan: how about you?
DecOlan: what moment changed you forever?

Brief pause. Typing. Then she pops out with something that jars me back to real life. The one where I'm supposed to hate her.

KnuckLise99: i guess . . . what happened at Freshman Fling.

DecOlan: let me guess. trust issues? hating the entire male species?

KnuckLise99: <<rueful smile>> something like that.

Once again, I have to steel myself, remind myself what I'm doing here. Annalise is *not* my friend. She is someone who can't be trusted. Someone who cornered my best friend's boyfriend when he was drunk and vulnerable, not caring that he had a long-time girlfriend. Talking with her like this, I've let my guard down. Almost. But no. I have to stay focused on my true mission: keeping Cooper far away from her. Even if I never get him for myself, I know one thing for certain. A girl like Annalise Bradley would only break his heart.

Still, there's one thing I would like to know.

If she regrets what she did.

DecOlan: would you change it?

DecOlan: if you could go back in time?

KnuckLise99: oh yeah. big time.

KnuckLise99: i'd see that asshole crying

KnuckLise99: and keep on walking.

CHAPTER 9

ANNALISE

Thursday morning, I'm lying in bed, semiconscious, bargaining with my alarm's snooze button for fifteen more minutes of sleep, when I hear my phone vibrate under my pillow. Groggily, I reach one hand out from under my covers. What I read makes me bolt up, wide awake. If I were a cartoon character, my head would hit the ceiling and be haloed by tiny revolving stars. It's an alert marked Urgent! from the Brass Knuckles fan page—a rare message from the band itself.

KNUCKLIES: WANT TO SING WITH THE BAND? WE'RE RAFFLING OFF THE EXCLUSIVE CHANCE TO SING ONSTAGE WITH VIGGO WITTS AT OUR UPCOMING BOSTON SHOW! RAFFLE TICKETS ARE $10; ALL PROCEEDS GO TO VIGGO'S CHARITY, CHANGING FACES, AN ORGANIZATION SUPPORTING CHILDREN WITH FACIAL DISFIGUREMENTS. THE LUCKY WINNER WILL RECEIVE TWO FRONT-ROW VIP TICKETS AND HELP SING A DUET OF "IDENTITY CRISIS." BE AT THE SHOPS AT THE PRUDENTIAL CENTER TODAY AT 4 P.M. TO ENTER! BONUS PRIZE FOR THE FIRST 500 PARTICIPANTS.

I blink, then read it again to make sure I'm not imagining things. OMG. OMG. OMG. Win VIP tickets? Be guaranteed to sing the duet with Viggo? Within seconds, Knucklies like Juniper77 and DaisyFlour84 are buzzing like crazy over the news, with rumors of everything from a surprise appearance of the band to the official release of "Inner Beauty" off their new album. Only one thought pops into my head. *I have to tell Declan.* My fingers trip over one another as I pound out a message to him in all caps at light speed, proper spelling be damned. Why oh why did he have to lose phone privileges for whatever he'd done? I only hope he's in front of his computer this early in the morning, since if I were homeschooled, I'd sleep late for sure.

KnuckLise99: DEC!!! BRASS KNUCKLES TIX GIVEAAWAY AT PRU CENTER TODAY!!! CHANCE TO SING IWTH BAND. WE MUST GO!!

I copy the text of the message from the band, so he can see what I'm babbling like an insane person about just in case he missed it. And then I wait, hoping for a reply. Gloriously, I see his username fill in and it looks like he is typing a reply.

DecOlan: holy cannoli!
KnuckLise99: don't say you're still grounded. there must be a way! do I have to come kidnap you??
DecOlan: lemme think . . .

I wait and wait and wait. What's taking him so long? Finally, he replies and what he types back knocks me off my knees.

DecOlan: yep! my parents are going to a homeschooling meeting then out to dinner. i think i can swing it without them knowing.

KnuckLise99: awesome!
DecOlan: ok. it's a date.

A date?
Gulp. A date.
Is that what I want?

As much as I've been longing to meet up with Declan, now that it's actually about to happen, I'm not so sure. Chatting online has been easy so far. Like somehow, I became a wittier, more charming version of my real-life self. What if in person, I turn into a conversational dud? Or we don't connect? Too late, I think of all the horrible things that can go wrong when two people finally meet face-to-face. Body odor and sweat stains. Bad breath and bad chemistry. Inept tongues and awkward gropes. Maybe it was better to be free from all that. Keep what we have perfect, just the way it is.

Am I really ready for a date with Declan?

***

Declan suggests we meet at the visitor's information booth in the center of the mall, and I go wake up my mom to ask for permission to go.

"Alone? Into the city?" She mumbles from under the covers, groggy from working the late shift.

"I'll get Maeve to come," I lie.

"You'll come home right after?" she says sleepily. "It is a school night."

I leave out the bit about meeting a boy there, since I know that would change everything. Knowing my mom, it'll be the same old spiel, *boys can't be trusted, boys are slimebags*, all the things I already know and don't really feel like hearing again.

Especially since this could be different. This *is* different. This is Declan.

Instead, she has to give me another kind of reality check. "You know, honey, the chances of winning are really slim, right?" she says gently. "I just don't want you to be disappointed . . ."

"I know. I won't be," I insist, even though I can tell she doesn't believe me.

"Okay, fine. Good luck," she says, giving me a kiss, and rolling over back to sleep.

Since I'll be coming straight from school, and this is now officially a date, I change into my best skinny jeans with my favorite Knucklies T-shirt. I blow out my hair, swipe some dangling silver earrings of Elena's that she left behind on her dresser, and even remember to bring some lip gloss.

There is just one problem.

Maeve.

What do I tell her? What will she think? I never actually told her about Declan, and now, it feels way too late without hurting her feelings. Maybe it would be better to tell her about him after we've actually met, anyway. See how things go. Make sure the whole thing doesn't turn out to be a disaster.

When I get off the bus, I find her waiting for me in our usual pre-school meeting spot by the front steps, trying to inhale a granola bar before first bell.

I take a deep breath. "Guess what?"

She peers at my bubbly expression through her glasses and hazards a guess. "Eva Winters caught the bubonic plague and classes are all canceled?"

"No, better," I insist. "Brass Knuckles is giving away two tickets today."

Her eyebrows arch in disbelief. "Really?"

"Yeah, at the Pru Center downtown. After school." I tell her all about how the winner also gets to sing a duet with Viggo Witts. "And I'm going to win. I can just feel it." I do a little spin and hug myself.

She snorts at my optimism. "You, plus every other equally delusional fan. What are the odds? One in 10,000? I can see you've really been paying attention in math." Maeve's commitment to pessimism has bonded us this year, but this particular time, her lack of faith annoys me. Plus, I've already heard this lecture from my own mother.

"I don't care. I just know I will. I have to." Don't they see this was all meant to be? The fender bender. Me, not getting the tickets. The concert giveaway. Winning front row seats, better than anything we would have scored on Ticketmaster or even StubHub. I will take Declan and get to sing with Viggo, and the two of them will both fall madly in love with me and fight over me, right up there on stage. I am going to just will this to happen. The power of positive thinking, right?

She purses her lips, like she is thinking hard, then grins apologetically. "Okay, fine. Clear eyes, full hearts, can't lose, right? I'll come. Double your chances, at least."

Wha-at?

"Don't you have practice?" I squeak in alarm, my voice peeling high, and I hope she doesn't notice. "You just made the team."

"I know. I can probably skip out, just this one time . . ." Maeve wags her granola bar at me. "Besides, I know you can't find your way to the mall without my superior navigational skills."

This was true. I'm directionally challenged, even using Google Maps.

"But won't your coach kill you?"

She shrugs. "Tamara can tell her I have a twenty-four-hour stomach bug or something. Or, I know! I'll say there's another

Jewish holiday. Tell her I have to go to services for . . ." she pauses, then snaps her fingers "Simchat Torah!"

"But I thought you and Maya Gomez are competing for a spot on the first string. You don't want to give her an opening."

Now she is eyeing me suspiciously, as if noticing for the first time my lip gloss. "Do you . . . not want me to come or something?"

"No!"

She doesn't buy it, her eyes drinking in my smoothed hair and silver earrings. "Okay, spill it. What's going on?"

"Nothing!"

"Then why do you look all Glamour Shots today?" She gestures vaguely to my earrings and my hair. "Class photos aren't until *next* week."

"I don't!" I protest vigorously, shaking my head, which only makes my earrings jangle louder, betraying me.

"Are you going with someone else?"

Damn! She knows me too well. "Um, no." I say, caught, stumbling over my words. I take a deep breath. I am busted. Might as well 'fess up. "Well, yes. Actually. Not going with exactly. More like meeting. But—"

"Who?" she demands, hurt, like I have another BFF stashed away somewhere.

"No one. Just this guy."

She is clearly taken aback. "A *guy*? An actual member of the male species? One you have not told me about?"

I regret all the times Maeve heard me swear off the XY chromosome for good. I stumble over my words. "He's just another Knucklie, and we're going to meet there to try and win tickets."

"Do I know him?" she demands.

"No, he doesn't go here." I try to sound casual. "I met him . . . on the fan page."

"I can't believe you're ditching me for some guy."

"I'm not!" I protest. "You have practice! And—"

Maeve gasps. "Wait. Is he in college? Is that why the big mystery? You little vixen—"

"No, he's our age. He's homeschooled actually."

She absorbs this information, then asks, "Is he hot, at least?"

Yes. "I don't know," I shrug. "I guess. I've only seen his picture."

She tires of my evasion and cuts to the chase. "Answer me this: Annalise Bradley, do you have any intentions of ever seeing this person naked? Yes or no?"

I blush against my will. *Naked?* I was counting on the fact that there was no risk of getting physical at all. "No! I don't know. I've never met him. We've been chatting online. That's all." The description is a betrayal; I know it, and she senses it.

"How long?"

"What?"

"How long have you been chatting with this mystery man?"

I hesitate. "Every night this week."

She snorts in exasperation. "Oh my god, Annalise. How could you not tell me this?"

"Sorry, Mom." In fact, it had been pretty easy to hide Declan's existence from my actual mother, who spied on my Lamebook account as one of my "friends," but hadn't wised up that everyone I know has moved on. Plus, lucky for me, she's been super-distracted lately, spacing out on basic stuff like replenishing my cafeteria account, which forced me to scramble for lunch money twice.

"What do you guys talk about?"

Human nature; the afterlife; the meaning of it all. "Just stuff."

"And now you're going to meet him?" Her eyes narrow in suspicion.

"At the mall." I emphasize the last word, knowing where this is heading. It's not like we haven't had a million school assemblies about predators chatting us up online. "In public. In front of a thousand people. Like you just pointed out. Seriously, Maeve. I mean, if he was making stuff up, why would he be willing to meet me?"

"Well, I'm just saying. Have you ever actually talked to him? Heard his voice?"

"Well, no . . ." The words tumble out of my mouth as I hastily explain. "He's grounded, and his parents took away his phone."

"So no FaceTime. Don't they have a land line?"

Hello, 1983? "I'm not—"

"What about Skype?"

"Oh my god, Maeve, I'm not Skyping him!" Thank god neither of us had ever suggested that. Then I'd have to worry if I had something in my teeth or a looming zit on my face every time we talked. Plus, the angle of my video cam distorts like a funhouse mirror, making my boobs look as big as my head.

"I'm just saying, how do you know anything he's told you is true? Don't you know the first rule of the Internet? Everyone lies on the Internet! My aunt says everyone on Match.com is an inch taller, five pounds thinner, and ten years younger than they are in real life."

"I've Googled him, Maeve. There's tons of mentions in the local papers. With pictures and everything."

There had been one, with the caption, Declan O'Keefe, 11, Homeschooled Boy Wins Worcester County Chess Tournament, that showed him looking a lot younger and endearingly scrawny, all elbows and ears. And another article, about homeschooling kids who meet up at some engineering club, that quotes his dad, Patrick, boasting about his brilliant son, Declan.

"Hmph." Maeve grunts, and I can tell she is giving in. A little. "Okay. But I'm going to call and check on you. I'm sneaking my phone into practice."

I nod assent, wondering where on earth she will stash it. Her shoe? Her sports bra?

She is silent, thinking.

"So are you taking him if you win tickets?" she finally demands. "Or me?"

Shoot. I hadn't thought of that. Having to choose between the two of them. I dodge the question.

"I thought you said I had no chance, remember?" I smile weakly, but she gives me a stern look, like she is on to me.

"I don't get it," she says finally, shaking her head. "You have Cooper Franklin all over you. You told me yourself. Why are you even wasting your time with some online geek?"

"He's not a geek." I say, regretting I had ever mentioned Cooper's behavior to Maeve. "And Cooper's like that with everyone. He'd flirt with a tree stump."

"He doesn't flirt with me," she says, her mouth twisting. "I guess I'm not even stump-worthy." Maeve is convinced that none of the preppie guys at our burb school get her dark humor and she's destined to be single until college.

"Maeve—"

"No, it's fine."

Maeve, even Maeve, who knows me better than anyone, still doesn't get it. With Cooper, with any guy at Dansville, I'll never know what they're really after. My body? My backstory? Or me? But with Declan, I know for sure none of those things matter. Our connection goes beyond the physical plane, it is pure.

So what if it's based entirely on pixels?

CHAPTER 10

NOELLE

Can I help it if I was totally caught off guard this morning?

It was practically dawn, for one thing. I was still in bed when I heard Annalise's message ping me. My mind was still sleep groggy. But I knew this day was coming. With all the online flirting we'd been doing, it was only a matter of time before she suggested a meet up, even though the distance between her and Declan was kind of a haul and he was supposedly still grounded. How could I say no without making her suspicious?

Panicking, I had texted Eva what to do and she responded immediately with her usual certainty. TELL HER YOU'LL MEET HER THERE! TELL HER IT'S A DATE. MAKE UP EXCUSE AFTER.

When I get to school, Eva stomps up to me while I'm locking up my bike, looking irate. I'm positive something has gone wrong. My chest spasms; whatever she's about to say can't be good. So far, she hasn't bothered to follow the online chats, but did she read that last comment about Amos? Or worse, have we been found out? Did Annalise figure out what we're—

She clutches my arm and glances around the courtyard to make sure no one else is listening. "Guess what I heard. Ethan says

Cooper was talking about Annalise, yesterday at lunch." Eva's older brother, Ethan, a junior, was on the lacrosse team, too; the lax guys all tended to sit together like a herd of cattle. "Saying he's going to ask her out. Today. The guys were giving him a hard time, but he was defending her."

She looks indignant that anyone would stick up for her nemesis, but I smile inwardly. It's one of the qualities I admire most in Cooper. He doesn't care what the masses think; he makes his own judgments. Does Annalise even appreciate that? Probably not. Or at least, not like I do.

"So, it's over." I shrug in defeat. Cooper is definitely into Annalise. What more can be done?

"It's *not* over," Eva says emphatically, jabbing me in the arm. "She's not going to say yes to Cooper. Not when she's all jazzed about meeting Declan at that concert thingie today. Good thing she's already taken."

I'm not convinced a date with Declan, the homeschooled Cyrano, will outshine an offer from the real-life Cooper, especially when Declan's about to stand her up big time. "Yeah," I say, "but how's she going to feel when Declan doesn't show?"

Eva dismisses my fears with a wave of her hand. "So, something came up, right? A family emergency. Stomach bug. Train derailment. She'll forgive him, I'm sure. Maybe we should send her flowers afterwards. Like, to apologize?" She beams, pleased with her brilliance.

I say I'm not sure, that maybe she won't buy it, maybe she won't forgive him.

"Look," she says, frowning. "Maybe you really *can't* handle this—" She stops herself short, like there's more she knows but is not saying. Why? I stare at her, wondering if she knows I already messed up once before, whether Tori has betrayed my confidence.

I mumble that I've got it under control.

"You sure? Because, I mean, I'm swamped with rehearsals and stuff. But I can take over if you can't."

My mind races in alarm as I imagine Eva going back and reading all the intimate conversation threads between me and Annalise—things that I'd never discuss with her. And then there is that last discussion, mentioning what happened with Amos. She'll hit the roof.

So I tell Eva it's fine, that I can do it. But there's one thing still bothering me. "What's the point?" I ask her. "Even if she turns Cooper down. He's still into *her*. Not me. Nothing's going to change that."

She smiles confidently and says brightly, "Hello, rebound? She turns him down, but who's there to comfort him? Who's there to hear him out? You are, Noey. You're always there for him, and he never sees it. But this time, that's going to change. After math class, we're going to march over to his desk and ask him to study with us after school for the test. That's easy enough, right?"

Easy like walking the plank. But Eva's confidence can be infectious, so I nod okay, even though my stomach contracts at the thought. Our plan is to casually tell Cooper we'll be studying at my house and ask if he wants to come, too. "And then when she turns him down, he'll come running to tell you all about it. It'll work. Trust me."

I want to trust her. I always have. It's all I know how to do.

***

Eva and I happen to arrive at the door to math class at the exact same time as Cooper.

"Hey, No," he says with a big lopsided grin that liquefies me. "Eva," he nods politely. I smile back, trying not to wince at his nickname for me. No—it's not hard to read the subliminal message of rejection tucked in there.

On the board, Ms. Pinella has written in big scrawling letters: MATH TEST TOMORROW. REVIEW CHAPTERS 1–7. While everyone else goes over the material, I study Annalise instead, noticing that she has made an extra effort today. She's wearing these long dangling earrings I've never seen before and blown out her reddish hair, all to dazzle the boy I've invented, who exists somewhere between her head and my laptop. I can see her anticipation in the way she holds her body erect, alert and poised for the events that lie ahead. I see Cooper, also dazzled, glancing her way, trying to whisper something to her, and she shakes her head and shushes him, as if she doesn't want to miss a single word of Mrs. Pinella's fascinating review.

Forty minutes that feel like forty seconds later, the bell rings and Eva mouths, "Ready?" I am anything but, even though she comes up behind me, puts a hand on my hip like we are doing the Bunny Hop at my cousin Frieda's wedding, and guides me right toward Cooper.

When I arrive at his desk, I realize, sure enough, he is already halfway though the same invitation to someone else.

Her.

" . . . study together after school?" Cooper is saying to Annalise, as I freeze, standing there awkwardly. But then I see her lips falter, and I feel sorry for him because I know what he doesn't: Poor Coop doesn't stand a chance because she already has epic plans after school today. With "Declan."

Sure enough, she turns him down flat. "Sorry," she frowns. "There's this giveaway for Brass Knuckles tickets at the mall. I'm going to try to win them."

Eva and I exchange looks of elation; our plan is actually working.

"Brass Knuckles?" Before Cooper can help himself, he blurts out. "They were on SNL last month, right? That lead singer's such a pretty boy . . ."

Annalise's whole body stiffens. "He is not. Like, he may be hot, but he doesn't care about superficial stuff. For your information, his charity helps kids born with messed up faces and stuff. He's all about keeping it real."

Cooper snorts something under his breath.

Eva slides into the conversation. "Cooper, you're an idiot. That band is awesome. I heart Viggo."

You do? I almost say. Since when does Eva love Brass Knuckles? Since when does she even know the lead singer's name? What is she up to? Annalise looks equally surprised, probably that Eva would actually agree with her on anything.

"Noelle!" She spins in my direction. "We should totally go try to win tickets too!" It's an Oscar-winning performance, like the idea actually excites her. I stare at her in confusion, startled by this turn of events. Once Cooper realizes Annalise is busy, won't he accept the invitation to study with us instead? Wasn't that the plan? Wasn't that *our* plan?

"Um, I dunno," I stammer, giving her a *look*. "There's no way we'll actually win. Shouldn't we just, um, study? At my place?"

But she just shakes her head at me meaningfully and says, "Come on Noey, don't be so uptight. We can study after. We definitely can't miss this. I'll tell Tori." And just like that, the decision is made.

Too late, I realize Eva's agenda is slightly different than mine. I know exactly what she wants—what she's always wanted. To be there in person to watch Annalise squirm. It's not enough to orchestrate it. She wants to watch it go down: Annalise getting stood up, her reaction when she realizes Declan isn't coming. It's become a show to her. Live theater. The sport of another's misfortune, like cock fighting or YouTube bloopers.

Cooper and Annalise are still sparring over the lead singer, oblivious to our standoff. "Doesn't the guy have, like blue hair?"

"Yeah, so?"

"And he sings like this?" He curls his lip, grabs a pen as a pretend microphone, and does a remarkably good impression of Viggo Witts.

Annalise is so pissed she's practically steaming like an espresso machine. "He sings nothing like that! He's got an awesome voice."

This is better than I expected. Things between them are falling apart in front of my eyes. Cooper is a lunkhead if he thinks he will score points with her this way. Maybe I have nothing to worry about. Even as his biggest fan, I have to admit, the boy has absolutely no filter. And he seems to finally figure that out, a beat too late.

"Look," he says, retreating. "I'll go with you, help you win some tickets. Then we can study at the mall. Grab some food? Sound like a plan?"

But she cannot be swayed. "Actually, I'm meeting someone else there."

"Oh, really?" Eva says, snaring Annalise in her Venus flytrap. "Who?"

Annalise looks like a child whose hand has been caught in the cookie jar. "A friend," she finally says.

Cooper appears crestfallen at this news.

"What's his name?" Eva presses.

"You don't know him," she says, her cheeks turning ever so pink. "He doesn't go here."

"So, how'd you meet?" Cooper asks, and I can't help but think that if he were an M&M, this time, he'd be green, only with jealousy instead of lust.

"Online."

"Oh, so it's like a blind date?" Eva gushes, pulling out an Altoid and popping it in her mouth. "That's so cute."

Cooper looks annoyed. "You're meeting some guy that you met on the Internet? Are you sure he's not a freak?"

"He's not a freak." Her face twists with annoyance, as if she has heard this before.

"How do you know?"

"I just . . . do. He's amazing. He's super smart and cool and he gets me. And, he gets Brass Knuckles." She glances at Cooper and I can see the dig makes him wince. But I am somewhat flattered to have my alter ego given such a rave review. Who knew I was amazing? Cooper, my lifelong crush, clearly doesn't think so, and my best friend Eva doesn't think so, but Annalise does. My torn loyalties inch back a sliver in her favor.

"Well, good luck," he says to Annalise, as the room begins to fill for the next period. "I hope you win."

Eva sticks out her lower lip and fake pouts. "Aren't you going to wish me luck too?"

Cooper swings his gaze to Eva. "Yeah, but somehow, Eva, I don't think you need it." I try to stifle a laugh as she frowns, not sure whether to take that as a compliment or an insult.

I make one last attempt to salvage the situation. "You could come along with us, you know." My words smack of desperation, I know, but what else can I do?

Cooper mentally weighs the options; joining us, but having to watch Annalise fawn over some other guy. "Nah, I'll catch you next time. Better hit the books." He shifts his book bag onto his shoulder and calls across the room. "Yo Tyler, man, wait up!"

Eva takes my arm and guides me toward the door, but not before she stops to wave her hand at Annalise. "See you there, A. Can't wait to meet this dream guy." And I'm left to wonder: Does Eva care at all about getting Cooper and me together, like she said? Or is she only out for one thing: revenge?

CHAPTER 11

ANNALISE

"WELCOME KNUCKLIES!"

When I finally arrive at the Prudential Center, it is packed. Beyond packed. It is like Black Friday and Christmas Eve and the line for Space Mountain, all rolled into one. I elbow my way through the mass of bodies, following the bright yellow banner directing me to the main atrium, where the giveaway will take place.

One good thing about this crowd—there's no way Eva Winters and her crew will ever be able to find me. I still don't get why she made such a big deal about coming. On what planet is she a Brass Knuckles fan? Planet PissMeOff, that's where. She still hasn't gotten over what happened last year, that's for sure. And I still can't get over the look of surprise on Cooper's face when I declined his study date. Like I was the first girl in all of humankind ever to turn him down. I would have felt bad if he hadn't gone and called Viggo a pretty boy and mocked his singing style, just like I predicted he would.

As I push my way toward the central court, I hear the familiar intro chords of "Identity Crisis," and for a second, my belly cartwheels and I think the rumors are true and the band is actually here, surprising us all with a live appearance. Then I come around to the front of the stage and realize it is just two chubby old DJs from the radio station sitting behind a table, with two ginormous speakers set up alongside them, blasting the recorded music. In front of them, a pit of girls my age in tight jeans and wedge heels, all wearing yellow wristbands, is writhing and spinning like a school of eels, mouthing along to the lyrics. I wonder if Juniper77 and DaisyFlour84 are here like they said they'd be. I've chatted with them for hours about Viggo's life story, but I realize I wouldn't recognize them even if I ran smack dab into them.

A huge line, set off by purple velvet ropes, snakes around the room. I find the end of it, and while I'm waiting, the song finishes up and one of the DJs announces that they'll be calling the winning number in about twenty minutes. When finally I reach the front, a woman in white jeans, a blazer, and a T-shirt that reads WXKS ROCKS! takes my ten bucks and efficiently cuffs me with a yellow wristband with the number 245674 printed on it. "Good luck," she says with a smile, handing me something rolled up in a tube. "Your poster. Don't lose it."

"Thanks," I say, grasping it carefully in my other hand so it doesn't get crushed and wading back into the throng toward the information booth, where Declan had said we should meet once we got our raffle tickets. Good thing we had a prearranged spot—I would never have found him otherwise in this madhouse. I fight my way there, worming my way upstream like a woebegone salmon.

"Annalise!" A loud voice calls out my name.

Declan?

I turn, realizing as I do that it can't be—it's the voice of a female. High-pitched. Shrill. Hateful. Eva. She and two of her cronies are coming up right behind me, waving frantically like we're besties, yellow wristbands also circling their wrists. Un-ignorable. How on earth did they find me? And why did I have to go and mention

Declan to Eva & Co.? Before that, our online relationship was all our own, safe from their prying eyes and the rumor mill.

We face off, and Eva smirks at me as if she knows something I don't.

I feel conspicuously alone. A big part of me is regretting that I hadn't told Maeve to skip practice and come be my second, like in *Grease* when Kenickie bashes his head and Danny has to drive Greased Lightning in the drag race. I should never have come here by myself.

"So, where's your fanboy?" she asks, flipping her long brown hair behind her ears.

"What?" I shout, making like I can't understand what she's asking, even though I do. Between the music blaring, the people screaming, and the bad acoustics, it's pretty impossible to hear anything.

"She said, where's your fanboy?" Tori repeats, raising her voice.

Good question. I scan all the bodies standing around the info booth, but I don't see Declan anywhere. Yet.

I make an exaggerated shrug, trying not to show my nervousness. "I'm sure he'll be here soon."

"We'll help you find him," Eva yells.

Tori peers into the crowd. "What's he look like?"

I'm about to describe Declan, but it's going to be tough to make myself heard. Instead, I just pull up his picture on my phone and point at it.

"Oh, cute," Tori says, grinning like a hyena and poking Noelle for confirmation. "Definitely pageant material."

Noelle looks briefly at the photo and just nods, too superior to actually speak to me.

The three of them scan the crowd while I stand there, trapped. I can't figure out why they're here. Does Eva no longer hate me, now that I have moved on to another guy and am no longer a threat to her and Amos? Or are they waiting around to see him so they can trash him, mock him? Part of me can't wait for him to get here, and part of me is dreading him showing up, not knowing what Eva has planned. I eye her suspiciously. Is she going to tell him that I tried to steal her boyfriend and not to hook up with me? Or am I just being paranoid?

A man in a black T-shirt and black jeans bounds up on the stage. "Hell-o Boston," he mouths into the microphone in a sexy British accent as the crowd whoops loudly in return. When I see who it is, I almost have a massive heart attack—it's Colin Dirge, the manager for Brass Knuckles! What's *he* doing here?

"Who's that?" Eva crinkles her nose as everyone around her roars in excitement.

"I'm Colin Dirge, the manager of Brass Knuckles, and I wanted to thank you lovely fans for turning out today. We are so thrilled to close up our first U.S. tour here in Boston, and thank you to WXKS for organizing this raffle benefiting Changing Faces, an organization that has deeply touched Viggo's life. I've popped by today . . ." He pauses dramatically and it feels like we all collectively hold our breath. What is he going to announce? Is the band really going to make a surprise appearance? ". . . to give you lucky fans a sneak peek at the first single to be released off our new album, *Mistaken Identity*. It's called 'Inner Beauty' and I think you're going to love it. Also, I have a surprise for you. If you check the back of your posters, there is an access code, which will allow each of you one free download of the song!" The crowd hollers and cheers, and everyone scrambles to make sure they still have their posters.

"And now here, it is. Take a listen," he says, beaming like a proud father, as the new song begins blasting from the loudspeakers.

You sparkle
You shine

Your cheekbones
Sublime.
But a pretty face
does not mean a pretty heart.
There's just no inner beauty
Where is your inner beauty?
Without some inner beauty
You're a perfect waste of time.

It's the same song that Declan had sent me, but something is different. I listen hard for a half a minute and then I figure it out: The original version was stripped down, raw and pure, while this one is more upbeat, more catchy, more commercial. An instant hit, guaranteed. There had been rumors swirling that the band was back in the studio this week reworking one of the songs, all obviously true. Although I had to admit, I liked the original slightly better; either way, the song was genius—never mind what that numbskull Cooper Franklin would say.

"Brilliant, right?" Colin smiles as the song wraps up and the crowd goes nuts. "And now, let me introduce DJ Dr. Groove, who will pick the lucky winner to come up on stage and sing 'Identity Crisis' with the band. So good luck! Thank you, Boston! We'll hope to see you all next week!" He performs some fist-pumping, palm-sliding handshake with the DJ, waves goodbye, and hops off the stage. I crane my neck like an ostrich to try and see where he is going, but he has already evaporated into the crowd.

"Thank you, Mr. Colin Dirge!" The DJ with the mustache gestures after him as the crowd roars again. "Are you pumped? Get those wristbands ready! We'll be picking a winner any minute now."

Where is Declan? I am getting panicked that he is going to miss the drawing. My mind races through the possibilities. Maybe he missed the train? Maybe his parents caught him trying to sneak out? Or maybe he is here, but waiting for me at some other information booth? Is that possible? Did he see me with Eva and her friends and get scared off? Or did he see me and not like what he saw in person? Did he take one look and go running in the opposite direction?

All three girls are looking at me, either in pity or, in Eva's case, a look of smug triumph I want to smack off her face. I want to look anywhere else, so I look up. Above us, on the jumbo screen, is a slideshow of the children from Viggo's charity, faces that are twisted and misshapen, and for a brief second, looking at those hollow eyes makes me feel petty and small for obsessing about my own stupid problems.

"Why don't you just, like, text him?" Tori is looking at me as if I am an imbecile not to have thought of this earlier.

"He can't text," I say in frustration, realizing as the words tumble out of my mouth how implausible they sound. "He's grounded. His parents confiscated his phone."

As if to contradict me, all of a sudden, my phone zings. Could it be Declan, finding a way to text me somehow? Even though I know it's impossible, my heart pounds and I grab it while the three of them watch me.

But no. It's just a text from Maeve.

MaeveRose: So?????

I shake my head, trying not to let my face reveal my disappointment, and shove it back in my pocket. "Not him."

Then the DJ's voice hums into the speaker. "Okay kids, this is the moment. One of you is about to win two front row tickets to the Brass Knuckles concert—and get to sing with Viggo Witts himself! Check those wristbands, because I am about to call out the winning number in 10 . . . 9 . . . 8 . . ."

The crowd chants along with him 7 . . . 6 . . . 5 . . . 4 . . . 3 . . . 2 . . . 1 . . . while I want to shout, Wait. You. Have. To. Wait. Declan will be here. I know he will.

But I don't and he isn't and then the DJ is reading out a series of random numbers: 2-4-1-0-2-9.

My heart falls. Twice. Just as I process that Declan is really not coming, that the winning number is not my number, that once again, my chance to meet Viggo Witts has slipped out of my fingertips, that once again, the guy I am waiting for has failed to show, I hear an ear-piercing, dream-crushing whoop erupt beside me.

"I won!"

CHAPTER 12

NOELLE

I can't believe it.

Eva is frantically waving her arm in the air and hopping up and down for joy and screaming, "Oh my god, that's me. That's me!" She turns and grabs Tori and me, and we instinctively embrace in a celebratory hug. Out of the corner of my eye, I see Annalise standing there. Alone. Excluded. Stunned.

I can tell from the look on her face exactly what she's thinking. Eva has won. *Eva.* Who probably couldn't even name a Brass Knuckles song if it were the Final Teen *Jeopardy!* question and $50,000 in college scholarship money was riding on her reply. Eva, who I know has come here just to see the look on Annalise's face when she got stood up by her phantom boyfriend. Annalise looks like she's been sucker-punched.

"Young lady, yes you, come on up here." The DJ points at Eva, and she scrambles through the parted crowd up onto the makeshift stage. The DJ, who has long dirty-blond hair and is wearing a button-down shirt that is only partly buttoned, asks her name and where she's from. She giggles out her replies. He asks if she is a Knucklie and she gushes that she is. Then he asks who she is going to take with her to the concert. What is she going to say? The three of us never discussed what we'd do if one of us actually won. Will she pick me—or Tori? Is one of us about to be odd girl out? Will it be me? Eva gazes over to where we are standing, like she is trying to decide between us. Then, she locks eyes with Annalise. She says, "I'm going to take my boyfriend, Amos," and I can hear the slight emphasis she puts on the words *my* and *boyfriend*.

"Is he here?" the DJ asks, scanning the crowd.

"No, he's at soccer practice." She smiles proudly, as if she had something to do with it.

"And are you ready to sing?"

She grins with the confidence of someone who, as a sophomore, just landed the plum role of Sharpay in *High School Musical*. "I will be."

"Well, I hope you two have a rockin' good time," he says, patting her on the back and guiding her toward the back of the stage. "And to all you fans, thanks for coming out today and helping to support Changing Faces. Enjoy your poster and free download, and keep on listening to WXKS, the number one rock station."

"Can you believe it?" Tori shrieks and grabs her phone to share the news with everyone she knows. I shake my head, looking over at Annalise. We watch as Eva dances toward us, a crisp white envelope clasped tightly in her hand.

"This is so amazing!" she says, still slightly dazed by her luck. "They said they'd even get me some backstage passes. See, Noelle, and you said we'd never win." She pulls out the tickets and Tori begins snapping shots of Eva holding them up to tweet with the world as she twirls around and fluffs her hair and babbles about how much she's going to practice and what she should wear and how this could be her big break like Courteney Cox.

I can see Annalise struggling with the sheer unfairness of it all, the desire to snatch those tickets out of Eva's unworthy hands. Then, as if Eva would take pity on her and change her mind, she asks, sort of pitifully, "So, you're definitely taking . . . Amos?" *Amos.* There is a moment of silence. Tori and I gape at Annalise, shocked she went there. Dared to say his name aloud. The word seems obscene, like she has no right to say it in Eva's presence.

Eva stiffens and glares at Annalise. "Well, he is my boyfriend. You know, the kind that actually exists." She looks over at Tori, who kind of snickers approvingly.

"Declan *exists*," Annalise replies. A pause. A sharp intake of breath. "He does."

"Riiight," Eva says, as she gives me a knowing look. "If you say so."

Annalise looks like she has been slapped across the face. I can see her fighting back tears. But I know and Eva knows she has no good comeback. No way to prove what she says is true. No physical evidence.

Without another word, Annalise turns and flees into the crowd.

I know this was the plan all along. What else did I think was going to happen? I know Eva would say I shouldn't feel sorry for her. Not at all.

So why do I feel so hollow inside?

CHAPTER 13

ANNALISE

I push my way through the mall, with only one thought going through my mind. Escape.

It was bad enough, standing there and watching Eva win the tickets that should have been mine, taking the spot on stage that could have been mine. And then, breaking down and groveling, actually asking her if she'd take someone else (me me me?) instead.

Pitiful.

Even if I offered to do her math homework from here to eternity, there was no way she'd give up this chance for me. And then worse, her accusing Declan of not even existing, implying that I'd made him up. I could tell by tomorrow, her version of the story would be all over the school and, once again, it would all start up again. Everyone would be staring, whispering, evading. Talking about me but not to me.

Declan exists! I want to shout. But where is he? Why didn't he come? I have no defense. All I have is a photo on my phone and some pretty words on a screen. And a connection that I know is real.

But all I can hear are Eva's words, echoing in my mind. My boyfriend, Amos. My boyfriend.

And against my will, my mind flashes back to that day, the way it felt to stand there, waiting, for someone who also promised to come.

Amos.

Whom I stumbled upon curled up in the hallway outside the Freshman Fling, on my way to the bathroom, all alone, because Maeve had started debating the stupidity of intelligent design with some fundie guy from her biology class. Amos, who had spiky dirty-blond hair and a trim waist and a ready smile. Amos, who had been dating Eva since practically the first week of freshman year. Amos, whose body was heaving almost like he was . . . crying.

Then he turned, and our eyes locked, and even though we really only knew each other from third period American History, I couldn't ignore that. His blue eyes were all watery and red, which you never see on a guy, especially not a guy like that. So I stopped and asked if he was okay. He muttered, "I'm fine," but it was obvious he wasn't and so I slid down against the wall beside him, not really knowing why. Up close, his breath reeked of alcohol, and he'd offered me a sip from a silver flash he pulled out of his jacket, but I shook my head. Eventually, he told me how he and Eva and gotten into a huge fight and how she had broken up with him. Then we heard the click of a teacher's heels coming toward us and, not wanting to be busted, we made our way down the hall.

Somehow, we ended up sitting alone on the west wing stairwell while he rehashed their entire relationship for me: how she was always getting on him for stupid stuff, and how he was sick of it, and how he was glad it was over. I felt exhilarated, honored that he was confiding something so personal with me. It made perfect sense after we talked for what seemed like hours, and his tears had dried up, that he turned to me, his breath warm, and slowly stroked a lock of my hair, and murmured, still sadly, "maybe, if I were with a girl like you instead," and leaned way in, as if he were about to kiss me. In the background, I could hear the thump of Brass Knuckles wafting in from the cafeteria, an unmistakable sign, telling me this was meant to be, and so I leaned way in too.

That's when Amanda Gerard and Tess McDonohue stumbled loudly into our stairwell, clearly looking for a place to sneak a smoke. "Whoops!" Amanda had giggled when she saw us there, causing us to jump apart like magnets that repel. Then, she gave us a serious double take, her eyes boggling and nudging Tess as if she might have missed us. "Sorry!" they cackled, although you could tell they weren't one iota, as they hastily retreated back inside.

Amos jumped up, knowing right away this would be bad, but I, stupidly naïve, didn't realize that. Not right away, anyway. All I knew was that somehow, the spell had been broken. The bubble burst. We stumbled to our feet and walked down the hall together, but instead of going inside to the dance, he told me he needed to head on home because he was hammered. He paused and looked at me and my face must have begged the question because he tugged on a curl and said, "Meet me tomorrow, 'kay? At the flagpole?" I smiled and agreed, and floated back inside to the dance. Even though it was only minutes, no, seconds later, I was greeted by these looks that made my stomach queasy. Of course Amanda and Tess had come back and told people that Amos and I were hooking up in the stairwell; of course someone had texted Eva the news; of course Eva called Amos and chewed him out for humiliating her.

But at the time, I knew nothing. I'd gone to sleep that night still the princess of my own fairytale, believing him, what he said, that he meant it, that he wanted to be with me, all of it. Until the next day at school, when I showed up where he had told me to meet him. At the flagpole. And I waited. And waited. And waited.

Until finally, I saw him, strolling slowly, casually, up the cement steps, aggressively not looking my way, his arm slung possessively around Eva, who was shooting death daggers at me. My heart dropped into my shoes and I wanted to fold up and die. All the truisms I'd overheard my mother saying to her friends on the phone ever since the divorce came rushing through my head: *men are dogs, men are cheats, men are liars.*

By noon, everyone knew what had happened the night before— or at least, Eva's version of the story. Which only got worse and worse, as the day progressed. How I had found him alone at the dance and tried to seduce him. How he'd gone along, happy to cop a feel. That we'd had sex, right there in the stairwell. That he was too drunk to remember any of it. How he came to his senses and confessed everything to Eva later that night, and she magnanimously took him back, because he truly loved only her, of course. And I realized it was all a lie, his supposed breakup, his tears, his murmurs, that he was playing me, right from the start.

Even though I tried to protest the truth, that nothing had happened, that he'd told me he and Eva weren't even together anymore, no one cared. Eva's friends whispered "home wrecker" and "man stealer" whenever I walked by, like I could ever do that, be that person, after I saw what my dad's affair put our family through. Even girls that I'd always been friendly with shied away, like I was toxic, contagious, while the popular guys leered at me knowingly like I was human trash, something to be used and tossed away.

At least school ended three days later, and I didn't have bump into Eva and her crowd for the rest of the summer, hanging out at the town pool or the Dairy Queen. With Maeve gone anyway, I begged Mom to let me escape, spending half the break at my grandma's house up in Vermont and the other half with my dad and his new family (the toddling terrors!) down in North Carolina. My mother, who was so good at scanning for damage inside other people's bodies, never once detected my own inner turmoil, and how could I tell her that I had become the thing she hated the most: the other woman.

After that, there was no way I was letting myself get burned again. Even by so-called nice guys, like Cooper. It was safer to just push them all away, the guys whose intentions were unclear, whose eyes lingered in the wrong places, who thought they knew who I was from a story they'd once heard. And Declan? I thought things would be different with Declan, who knew me from the inside out, rather than the other way around. But have I been all wrong about him, too?

I push through shoppers strolling with their bulging shopping bags, tears now streaming down my face, blurring my vision. Storefronts flash before my eyes: Sephora. Starbucks. Barnes & Noble. Cheesecake Factory. A shopapalooza blur. I flee down the escalator and through the doors. All of a sudden, I see someone pivot into my path and before I can stop myself, we collide. I feel something cold and wet all over my shirt and neck and someone yelling, "bloody hell!" I rub the salty tears from my eyes and taste . . . chocolate.

I read the glowing red sign above us and realize I have run smack dab into some grown man, and creamy brown ice cream has splattered all over his black T-shirt and jeans, and my favorite Brass Knuckles T-shirt. And he sounds quite pissed. "Why don't you bloody watch where you're going!" he hollers in an accent that would be charming, if it weren't so angry.

"I'm sorry. I'm so sorry." I freeze, not knowing what to do. Then I look up at his twisted lip and realize who I have just crashed into.

Colin Dirge.

CHAPTER 14

NOELLE

Eva obviously doesn't feel the same way. Long after Annalise has fled, she is still doubled over in shrill laughter. "Can you believe it?" she says, gasping for air. "She's defending that her imaginary boyfriend exists—the one we made up." Tori is infected with the absurdity of the situation and the two of them snort laugh for awhile, leaning on one another for support, wiping tears and snot from their damp faces.

Meanwhile, I feel empty. Deflated. Talking online to Annalise never felt hurtful, even talking about Amos. But now, seeing her in person, seeing her reaction to Declan's absence, the reality of what we are doing hits home. Hard. A crowd of dejected fans presses around us, streaming out of the area. More than one gives Eva a resentful look, but she is oblivious. "Let's get out of here," Eva finally says, composing herself.

Tori links her arm through Eva's and asks, "Pinkberry?" As if nothing is wrong. As if we should just go grab smoothies and hang.

I say I am leaving and turn to head home. This air is pulsing with body heat and I feel like I am going to be sick.

"Noelle, don't go!" Eva says. "What's the matter?"

I can't disguise the hot accusation in my eyes.

"What?"

"I . . ." What now? I pause, and try to pick my words carefully. I tell Eva I think that was harsh. That this game is getting out of control.

Her dark eyes widen innocently. "Why? It's not my fault she made up a fake boyfriend and got busted when he didn't show." She shakes her head, as if she can't quite believe it herself.

"Come on, Eva," I say quietly. Is *that* the story she plans to share with the school? I can't believe I am sticking up for Annalise Bradley, but someone needs to. "It's enough. We should quit while we're ahead."

Eva looks surprised that I am daring to defy her. When was the last time I contradicted her? Never? She looks at Tori, who rolls her eyes, as if I'm the one being lame. Before Tori came along, Eva always used to stick up for the underdog: usually me, but others, too. When did she change?

"Okay," Eva says slowly, pulling out her phone. "So say we want to quit. How, exactly, do we do that? Do you want to just dump her, Noelle? Tell her 'Declan' is really sorry, but he's met someone else? I can do that."

And that's when the reality of what we have set in motion is clear—we, no, I am trapped. If Annalise finds out the truth, what we've done, how we could publicly humiliate her, she will be crushed. But if we just stop the game, pretend Declan has had a change of heart, cuts it off, she will be equally crushed. I knew this was a bad idea. Knew that I never should have gone along with it. Why did I? And now, I am the one stuck cleaning up Eva's mess. As usual.

"No," I whisper, knowing I will handle it. I will apologize for Declan's no-show, come up with something convincing. And then what? Figure something out. Some way out.

"Okay. So we continue." She starts typing something into her phone. Too late, I realize what she is doing. Remotely logging into Declan's account.

Why didn't I change the password when I had the chance? Now it's too late. There's no telling what Eva will do. When she is finished, she holds up the message for Tori and me to see.

A, So, so sorry I missed you today. Emergency! I'll explain later. Please forgive me. Did you win??? xoxo Declan.

CHAPTER 15

ANNALISE

After I apologize a million times, Colin finally stops muttering "bugger," and says, "s'okay," looking a little embarrassed by his initial outburst. He takes the gob of white paper napkins in his hand and attempts to wipe the chocolate stains off his face and shirt. "I'll buy you another," I offer, reaching into my purse and pulling out some dollar bills. I try to push them into his hand.

"No need," he says, rejecting my money, and the bills flutter to the floor. I kneel to pick them up, shoving them in my pocket, and he offers me a chivalrous hand up. It is too much, this simple gesture of kindness, and I burst into tears again.

"Please luv, there's no crying over spilt ice cream," he says. He notices the band poster clenched in my hand, now dented and spotted with brown smears. "Or over lost concert tickets," he adds. "Is that it?"

I nod, yes, then shake my head, no. It is more than that.

"They'll be around next year, I'm sure. Or, you'll fancy some new band by then."

Why do all these grownups keep saying that? I shake my head vehemently. Never.

He sighs to himself. "Trust me, luv, cry over Darfur, if you must, but not bloody Viggo Witts."

At this, I just wail louder.

He looks around, anxious to move on, but unwilling to leave a sobbing girl crying alone at the mall. "Where's all your mates? Are you here alone?"

"Someone was supposed to meet me here. This boy . . ." It's all I can muster. He shakes his head and offers me one of the unused napkins to cry into and waits there patiently until my snot has turned the napkin all soggy. When I've finally recovered enough to regain my wits, I can't help but wonder what he's doing here. He was obviously in London doing post-production work on "Inner Beauty" all week, but shouldn't he already be with the rest of the band in Las Vegas, for this weekend's Teen Pick Music Awards? "Why are you in Boston?" I blurt out. "Aren't you supposed to be on your way to Vegas by now?"

He gives me a double take, like I'm some crazy stalker for following basic industry news.

"The TPMAs?" I stammer, knowing the band is strongly rumored to win, which means they have to show. "Isn't sound check, like, tomorrow morning?"

"Huh," he chuckles uncertainly, looking around as if for assistance. Mall security, maybe. "Do I need a restraining order here?"

"Johnny Cape tweeted he had a bad night at craps at the Hard Rock," I say, referring to the band's drummer. "I thought you were all out there already."

"Ah, right you are," he says, relaxing a teensy bit. "I stayed a bit late to tweak things. My flight had an eight-hour layover at Logan. Figured I'd pop in on an old chum for lunch, and since I was right here, check the turnout."

I nod; it makes sense. He'd once told *Rolling Stone* that too many music execs get out of touch with their fans, and that he likes to sneak up into the cheap seats occasionally to watch a show. Then, something else clicks in my brain. "Oh! You mean, Roger Fenley?" I'd read in some industry magazine profile eons ago that Colin and Roger had been roommates at the London College of Music, and Roger Fenley was now a tenured professor at the Berklee College of Music.

"Right again," he says slowly. "Roger. How'd you know that?" He eyes me, and I can tell he is thinking that he really *does* need a restraining order.

Now I am blushing like crazy. "No, it's just, I read it somewhere, I guess. I'm sorry. I'm just a big fan of your work."

"Well, thanks, luv." He looks around again, as if trying to find an invisible escape hatch to escape. But there is no way I'm letting *that* happen.

"Although, I have to say, I kind of liked the first version better," I blurt out, desperately trying to keep his interest in our conversation alive. "Of 'Inner Beauty.' It was less auto-tuned."

His head swivels sharply in my direction. "You think so?" He looks at me critically, as if I've finally said something noteworthy. I beam, not believing I am standing here in a discussion with *the* Colin Dirge. Then he frowns. "Wait. How did you hear the earlier version?"

Busted. I stammer out something about an unauthorized copy online that a friend slipped to me.

"Bloody little buggers," he shouts, slapping his thigh in anger, and then interrogates me on the little I know about the bootlegged copy. Eventually, his eyes soften and lock on mine. "Well, I happen to agree with you, but the president of the label thought otherwise."

"Not that it was bad," I say hastily. "It was still amazing. Viggo's voice, his lyrics . . . he's a genius."

"Right," he smiles knowingly, as if he's heard this all before. "Plus, he's easy on the eyes, eh?"

"It's not that," I protest. "Not for me." My voice lowers to a whisper. "His music. It just says something to me. I can't explain it. That's why I wanted to meet . . ." My face crumples as I think again about Eva winning tickets, singing with him, Eva, who doesn't even—

I sniffle a little and try to blink back my tears by staring furiously ahead.

"Oh, sod it," he says suddenly, whipping out his cell phone and wallet and pulling a business card out from inside. "What's your name, luv?"

I hesitate for a moment, not sure why he is asking.

He flashes me an impatient look. "Come on, no more blubbering. Quickly. Before I change my mind."

"Annalise Bradley," I reply, confused, as he types that into his phone.

"Right. Now, text that number on my card a day before the performance, and remind me. I'll have two tickets waiting for you at Will Call."

And he hands me his business card, which should read "Fairy Godmother" but instead says simply, Colin Dirge, Manager, and a cell phone number.

"Really?" I whisper in disbelief. I'll be there, in the crowd, and maybe Viggo will bypass Eva and pick me to sing instead, you never know. "Thank you so much, Mr. Dirge—"

"Colin—" he says with an involuntary shudder. "Mr. Dirge is my father."

But I can't call him that. "You don't know—this means so much."

He smiles at me. "Well, I was fifteen once. Couldn't get backstage passes to meet Oasis, but my cousin was a roadie, snuck me in, eventually got me a job in the business. Good times. My parents thought I was throwing my life away. And here I am. Not like it's all sunshine and lollipops, mind you."

He grins furiously and it hits me—here is a career not limited by my boobs. Forget math tests, and snotty girls, and well, high school. This, this is the real deal. Maybe I could do what he does someday, discover and promote musicians I love, hang with radio DJs, organize ticket giveaways, oversee worldwide tours. It's so obvious, so perfect, it's almost enough to force a slight curve to my lips.

"That's the spirit!" He pats me on the back, completely unaware he has just triggered a life-altering epiphany here at the mall. "Right now, off you go. Just remember. You tell no one, this never happened, understand? I can't go getting tickets for all your mates."

I do. Sort of. I stare at the card, mesmerized, nodding my head and planning to text Maeve as soon as is humanly possible. She's never going to believe this.

He turns and heads back to the counter, ready to order another cone. "Fantastic stuff," I hear him murmur as I pull out my phone, which has just pinged. "Best thing in the whole bloody States."

CHAPTER 16

NOELLE

I don't talk much to Eva or Tori the whole train ride back. When I get home, I hear voices. Loud ones, in the living room, coming from my mom. And soft, pleading ones from my dad.

"You didn't think to consult me first?" My mother sounds harsh, angry, wounded.

"Elise," he says in a firm voice I've rarely heard my dad use. "You know I just couldn't take another day under that jackass."

"That's what grownups do, John," my mother snaps. "They suck it up. For their families."

"What, I have to have the dignity sucked out of me? The life? Just take the abuse? Never take a stand for myself? So we can still afford fancy Key West vacations and your Botox injections?"

What are they talking about? What's going on? My mother does *Botox*? I walk into the room and hesitate by the door. The two of them are squared off in anger; neither one notices me standing there.

"You really think that's why I'm upset? You think I'm that shallow? We have responsibilities. Obligations. You don't just make impulsive decisions without talking it through. With your partner. This affects me, too."

"I have thought about it. Did you ever think about the message I've been sending to Noelle? Did you ever think of that? That it's okay to be bossed around like that? She saw it firsthand, this summer."

At the sound of my name, I kind of clear my throat. They both start, finally noticing me standing there. "What's going on?" I ask nervously.

My mother whirls and glares at me, as if I had something to do with it. "Your father just up and decided to quit his job, that's what. In this economy. Without so much as another offer."

Gulp. Maybe I did have something to do with it.

I look at my dad to see if it's true, and he nods at me. His eyes locking with mine, as if to say, let's keep this just between us. "I gave notice. But don't worry, honey. We'll be fine. Your mother's paycheck will cover us until I find something else. We'll just cut back on a few of the extras, that's all."

"Hmph," my mother snorts as I scan her wrinkle-free forehead for frown lines.

Go Dad! I want to shout, secretly proud that he'd finally stood up to his jerk boss. It couldn't have been easy for him. Why couldn't my mom see that?

"Well, if anyone cares about my opinion, I say Dad did the right thing."

My mother turns to me, her perfectly glossed lips pursed, furiously containing herself. "Noelle, could you please go up to your room? Your dad and I need to continue this discussion. Privately."

***

I escape upstairs and shut the door, not wanting to eavesdrop on the rest of their conversation. But it doesn't work. I can still hear the raised voices shouting below. It makes me twitchy when my parents fight, always nervous that one of them will just storm out, never to return. That happens, doesn't it? I mean, look at Annalise's parents. I know they split up, from the little she's said, although she hasn't told me exactly why. Was it money? One too many arguments? One wrong word that can never be taken back?

The phrase my dad had used downstairs is still ringing in my ears: *the message I've been sending to Noelle?*

Me.

I know exactly what he meant. The message that you have to stick with people, even the ones who make you feel like garbage. Out of inertia. Or fear. But maybe that's not true. Because look at my dad. He did it. Quit. Just like that. I can't believe it really was because of me, because of what I had said. What do I know? I'm just a kid. Still, my dad's actions embolden me. If he can stand up to his bully boss like that, why shouldn't I stand up to Eva, who was supposed to be my friend but lately feels more like my frenemy?

A flicker of rebellion sparks inside me. I know exactly what I have to do. I click onto the account settings and carefully change the login and password; then I log into the e-mail account Eva set up that first day and do the same.

I set the password to: Mistaken_Identity.

Click. Now, my decision can't be vetoed ever again.

I finally have the nerve to check my messages, and sure enough, Annalise had replied to Eva's fake note of apology on behalf of Declan. I almost don't have the nerve to read it. The image of her, running sobbing through the mall, ticketless and abandoned, is still replaying on a loop in my mind. What if the apology didn't work, and she's going to start berating me for standing her up?

I sigh. I can't avoid this forever. I click on her message to open it. But to my surprise, Eva's words seem to have done the trick, because Annalise seems positively chipper.

KnuckLise99: Dec, r u ok??? You won't believe what happened!!
DecOlan: what? u won?

I know that can't be it. But what could have possibly changed her mood between now and then?

KnuckLise99: no. the most amazing thing! but first what happened 2 u? what was the big emergency?
DecOlan: sorry i had to bail. it's all on me. my parents meeting was canceled. they came back when i was leaving. close call.
KnuckLise99: oh no!

I feel sick telling more lies, for stringing Annalise along, but what can I do? For now, I am trapped. If only there were a way Declan could just fade out gradually, avoiding heartache and betrayal. Move overseas. Or spend a year in juvie. Or even better, if only I could kill him off, like a minor character on a soap opera. Freak skiing accident in the Alps? Open elevator shaft? Killer bees? Annalise would be devastated, of course, but she'd move on eventually. But then, of course, the two of us would never get to speak again.

DecOlan: what's your news?
KnuckLise99: i didn't win . . .
KnuckLise99: <<suspense>>
DecOlan: lol . . . on edge of seat.
KnuckLise99: <<suspense>>
DecOlan: tell me, you big tease!
KnuckLise99: i bumped into Colin Dirge!!! literally.

Colin Dirge? I rack my brain. All my studying pays off. Right. Band manager.

DecOlan: yeah?! and?

KnuckLise99: he's leaving me two tickets at Will Call! <<happy dance>>

DecOlan: what? why?

KnuckLise99: we got to talking about the Inner Beauty track u sent. they remixed it and i told him i liked the original better. i dunno. i must have impressed him.

DecOlan: atta girl!

KnuckLise99: so u see it's all thanks to you. so you are so coming with me.

DecOlan: <<groan>> you know i can't.

KnuckLise99: what are you, under house arrest?

KnuckLise99: forever?

DecOlan: not forever. don't be mad.

KnuckLise99: <<pouting>> then tell me why. u never did. you owe me.

This time, at least, I am ready. I'd been racking my brain since the start what might have gotten Declan in trouble, bad enough to be grounded, sympathetic enough not to freak her out. Then I realized, the answer was staring me in the face. Right from my own life history. It was hands down the worst thing I had ever done. I still had mounds of guilt over it, even though I was only nine when it happened and my mom has sworn she has forgiven me by now.

DecOlan: got in a dumb fight w/my mom. shoved her. she fell. hurt her wrist. broke it. cast for six weeks.

KnuckLise99: OMG. that's awful.

DecOlan: i swear, it was a total accident. i feel sick over it. my punishment was loss of phone and to stay around the house until she gets the cast off.

I hold my breath, waiting for her to reply. Will she believe it? How will she react? Have I bought myself some more time? How much? I wait, hoping to see the signs that she is writing a reply. Nothing.

DecOlan: do u hate me?

KnuckLise99: no, it just reminds me. when i was eleven, i threw some stupid CD at my sister. scratched her cornea.

DecOlan: ouch.

KnuckLise99: she was fine. milked it for sympathy. made me feel wretched.

DecOlan: did she forgive you?

KnuckLise99: eventually.

DecOlan: so you don't get along?

KnuckLise99: we've just always been total opposites.

DecOlan: how so?

KnuckLise99: you know how i said high school isn't really all pep rallies and prom committee? for my sister, it was.

DecOlan: gotcha.

KnuckLise99: plus nothing ever bothers her. not even my dad—

She stops writing. The screen reads KnuckLise99 is replying. But the words take a long time to come.

KnuckLise99: he left us for someone half his age. elena forgave him.

DecOlan: but you didn't?

Again she doesn't write back immediately, and I wonder if I have asked too much. When she does reply, she changes the subject.

KnuckLise99: look don't worry about the concert. i'll take Maeve. we'll hang once your mom is better. ok?

DecOlan: i'll make it up to you.

KnuckLise99: yeah right. what could possibly compare to a Knuckles concert?

DecOlan: our first date.

And then I describe it for her, a hazy Hallmark card come to life: a sunset picnic down at the beach, with chocolate-covered strawberries and lobster rolls; the crash of the waves and the smell of the salt air; the wind in our hair and the sand between our toes. Lying back, pressing flat onto the woolen blanket, holding hands as the wily seagulls circle slowly. Dashing into the waiting ocean, letting them steal our unattended crumbs. The date is easy enough to describe. I've only pictured myself and Cooper on it about a million times before.

CHAPTER 17

ANNALISE

"I hope you're all ready," Ms. Pinella says, with only a touch of a sadistic smile, as she passes the test papers out to the class. Blargh. From the moment I walked into the room, I knew this wouldn't end well. I am so not ready for this. Out of the corner of my eye, I can see Eva, whispering to slander queen Amanda Gerard, then smirking at me.

My face starts to burn. I know what she's doing. Telling Amanda what happened yesterday at the ticket giveaway. How Annalise Bradley was a fool, waiting for some guy she met online who never showed. Or worse, pretending to have a boyfriend that didn't even exist and getting busted. I'd been such a complete lunatic, crying when he didn't show, hysterically running through the mall, although if I hadn't, I never would have crashed into Colin Dirge and scored tickets. After talking to Declan last night and clearing everything up, I felt so much better, I'd almost forgotten what was still waiting for me. This.

I glance over at Eva, knowing there is no way to stop her from spreading stories and making me look like an idiot. Are the glances and mean comments from last year going to start up all over again?

What if it never ends? What if she won't let it? What if everyone believes her?

I want to get up and leave, but there is no escape. Beside me, Cooper gives me an inquisitive look but I dodge his probing gaze and hug my hoodie tightly around my body. Then, the bell rings and the room quiets as everyone anxiously flips over the exam. Cooper hunches over his paper, his pencil scratching away. My eyes go blurry as I study the first test question.

Calculate the correct answer: If Declan lives 40 miles west of the city in Worcester and I live 20 miles south of the city in Dansville, how long would it take to get to his house, walking five minutes over to the station, then traveling 50 minutes by commuter rail to South Station and taking an hour-and-three-quarters train ride to his home, then walking 10 blocks at a rate of 5 miles an hour?

No, Ms. Pinella's test doesn't actually include this particular question. But I realize it's the only one I want to solve for X. That's it. I'm doing it. Today. I'm going to just go and finally meet Declan, face-to-face. The way he described our romantic first date still sends shivers down my spine, but why wait weeks until his grounding is over? If Declan can't come to me, I'll go to him. Track down every O'Keefe family within the Worcester city limits if I need to. Plus, if I can come home with a photo of the two of us together, it'll prove to Eva and whoever else she blabs to that Declan really does exist. That I'm not just making him up.

The more I think about it, the more I like the idea. I *can* do it. My mom is working the swing shift today, so she won't even be home until midnight. I'll go see him after school, pop in on him in person, surprise him. I'm sure if I can tell his parents the whole amazing story of how I was given the tickets, they will relent and suspend his grounding for this one night. If I plead with them, make my case, okay, put them on the spot, how can they say no? And when I show up at the concert on Declan's arm, even Eva will have to admit to the world she was dead wrong.

"Ten more minutes," Ms. Pinella announces, gently jarring me back to reality.

Crap. I have made little to no progress on this test. I quickly scratch in a few answers, skipping the ones that are too hard. Maybe I should have spent more time studying last night after I got home from the mall instead of chatting away with Declan for hours, while listening to the new version of "Inner Beauty" on repeat. I see Noelle Spiers, who probably did spend the rest of the night studying, finish the test early, get up, and saunter out of the room, glancing back smugly at the rest of us.

The bell tolls, indifferent to my cause. Cooper spies my test paper and gives me an odd look, noticing I have left the back page mostly incomplete. I quickly turn it over and shove it into the pile making its way up towards the front of the room. I can't think about it right now. Or him.

Ms. Pinella's sensible heels click on the tile floor as she circles the room; last call for dawdlers. As I rush out the door, I can hear Eva pleading with her for, like, one more second, and am pleased when she gets firmly denied.

***

"How much longer?"

I pull the earbuds out of my ears and squint at the route map. "Three more stops."

Maeve and I are squished in the back row of a Friday afternoon packed commuter train rumbling toward Worcester, listening to "Inner Beauty" for probably the seventy-eighth time in the last twenty-four hours, but who's counting? When I told her about yesterday's mall fiasco and my plan, she insisted on coming along, since there's no practice on Fridays anyway. I'd had to dip even further into my boob reduction kitty to buy two train tickets instead of one, but it was totally worth it to have Maeve along as company for the long ride.

"You sure I look okay?" I ask nervously. She'd taken one look at what I was wearing and insisted we stop by her house to give me a quick makeover, swapping out my band T-shirt for a daring cropped purple top from her closet and a pair of her skinny jeans so tight I could barely breathe.

"Positively fetching," Maeve says mockingly. "Samantha thought so."

Maeve's little sister had gasped in appreciation when I had emerged from Maeve's bedroom, then told me I had to sign up for this awesome online contest her friends were all doing—that turned out to be Tori's stupid *InstaHotOrNot* beauty pageant. Maeve and I had simultaneously groaned before Maeve hurled a pillow at Samantha's head and forbidden her to enter.

The conductor comes on the loudspeaker and announces our stop is next.

"Do you think I should have brought something?" I ask nervously, as the train's brakes begin to squeal in protest. My mother is a firm believer that you never show up at someone's home without a casserole or a bouquet of flowers.

"Like what?" She arches an eyebrow. "A nice Bordeaux?"

I shrug, feeling silly. "Guess not."

"Your presence is the present," she says grimly, rising to her feet.

We jump off the train and I study the street signs, totally disoriented by the unfamiliar surroundings. Never in my life have I been to Worcester. Now that we are actually here, my stomach is tied in knots of excitement. In a few more minutes, I will be face-to-face with Declan. I glance up at the sky, which was clear and blue when we boarded the train but now has dark clouds rolling in. Just what I need. A freak thunderstorm, so I can show up on his doorstep looking like a drowned rat.

"This way," Maeve directs, and I follow her lead. We are skipping excitedly down the sidewalk when a beat-up brown car approaches us, then slows down, pulling close to the edge of the street. A weasely faced boy, with a black baseball hat covering his greasy hair, hangs out the window. "Hey, ladies? How ya doing?"

I freeze, looking straight ahead, and Maeve answers with a clipped, "Fine."

"You lost? Need a ride?" he asks, shooting a look over at the driver, another boy whose sideburns and facial fuzz make him look seventeen-going-on-thirty-five. "Anywhere?"

Maeve shakes her head firmly, crossing her arms across her chest. "Do we look like we need a ride?" The car inches alongside us, spewing exhaust, and even though it is broad daylight, the empty street suddenly feels ominous.

He eyes me up and down, and I suddenly regret that Maeve talked me into this hoochie mama outfit, wishing I were back in my baggy Knucklie T-shirt, wishing I hadn't left my hoodie at home because it was so warm today. "How about you, Red? You more friendly than her?"

When I don't answer, his smile twists into something ugly. "Nice rack," he leers at me, and my mouth goes cotton ball dry.

Maeve cuts in. "Hey! Get lost, a-hole!"

I hear the driver curse at us as the car peels off. I am just relieved they are gone, but Maeve angrily snatches a rock off someone's driveway and hurls it after the bumper, using her spiking arm. She grunts with satisfaction as the stone sails through the air, and I crack a hesitant smile. *Clunk.* Impressively, she actually manages to nick the rear tire.

Her look of triumph changes to holy-crap panic as the car's driver suddenly slams on its brakes. Maeve grabs my hand and practically drags me down the street and around the corner, our feet pounding down the pavement, not daring to look behind us, sick with fear. We stumble through someone's backyard, where Maeve spots a child's playhouse and we clamber inside. My heart thumps like crazy as we huddle together, bent over at the waist, trying not to stomp on the princess pink plates and teapots belonging to some little girl who has yet to discover this darker side of gender relations. I try to speak but Maeve puts her fingers over her lips to shush me. We wait there for what seems like an hour, but is probably just ten minutes, and don't hear a thing.

We eye each other. Are they gone? Eventually, Maeve unfolds herself from the playhouse and brushes herself off, peering up and down the street. "All clear," she declares. But I am still frozen inside, shaken at the guy's creepy comments, feeling violated by his eyes. Why is it always me? Maeve doesn't take anyone's crap, but she also doesn't have to deal with guys leering at her like that, commenting on her body the way I do. I'd trade places with her in a second.

"Come on," she says impatiently. "You coming or not?"

I shrug, hanging back, the whole thing making me question why we'd ever come, reminding me what I already knew. What if Declan just seems perfect on paper? What if he is no Prince Charming, but instead a Prince Hans? What if like all boys, underneath, he is just another creep? Am I making a huge mistake?

She looks back in at me, assessing my shaking shoulders. "That guy was a loser. Seriously. Forget what he said. This is why you don't go to Worcester, right?"

I exhale a little laugh and smother my doubts. No. He is nothing like these morons. I *know* Declan. I know him. I know that he struggles between his love of science and his belief in a higher power, that he thinks reality TV has brainwarped our generation, that his favorite word in the English language is checkmate. I know that he hates public speaking but loves swimming in the ocean, the Lord of the Rings trilogy, and his family.

And possibly, someday, me.

"Let's go." I climb out and follow her back down the street, and we rehash the story, this time making fun of the boys' goofy faces and bad teeth, and I say I can't believe she has such good aim, and Maeve admits she almost crapped her pants when that car slammed on its brakes.

By the time we arrive on Declan's street, our mood has brightened. Maeve grabs my hand, double-checking the address I had pulled off the web and written on my palm: 43 Runyon Road. Finding it was easy—I searched for Declan's dad's name on whitepages.com, and luckily, there was only one Patrick O'Keefe in all of Worcester.

"This is it."

We stop in front of the modest brown ranch home. The lawn is neatly trimmed; the early fall leaves already raked away. To my relief, it looks like your typical suburban tract home. No crazy cult compound, after all. No barbed wire. No barking pit bulls. Two flowerpots of orange marigolds dot the doorstep.

Still, I linger. What if—?

"We didn't come all this way to admire the landscaping, did we?" Maeve pushes her glasses back up her nose. "Moment of truth," she says, shoving me toward the front door.

I nervously smooth my hair, hoping he's happy to see me, hoping I don't have anything stuck between my teeth, hoping he is all I have built him up to be.

We ring the bell, and wait. A few seconds pass and we hear voices inside, arguing over who should respond. Finally, we hear footsteps shuffling toward us, a male voice sighing, "Got it."

The front door opens, and I see him through the mesh screen door. My heart leaps. It is him. Definitely Declan.

Declan peers out through the screen at us. He is just as I'd imagined him, wearing a faded Star Wars T-shirt and a pair of loose blue jeans. A smile spreads over my face. I clear my throat, trying to gather my thoughts and what exact words to say.

He glances briefly at me, his dark eyes showing no sign of recognition. None at all. I could be a third-grader hawking Girl Scout cookies or a Hari Krishna showing up to recruit his soul for the afterlife. My smile falters as his gaze floats over to the left of me, and his face breaks into the beam I'd been expecting. The one I'd come all this way for. The one that was supposed to be for me.

"Maeve?" Declan says in complete disbelief, flinging open the screen door with an ear-piercing squeak. Then, he goes and gives Maeve the eager welcome that by all rights should have been mine. "Is that *you*?"

CHAPTER 18

NOELLE

The math test is a breeze, even though I hadn't gotten any studying done last night, between our little field trip to the mall and spending the night winning back Annalise's affections. I duck out early after handing it in, and spend lunchtime in the library, mainly because it's the last place on the planet Eva and Tori would think to go. After what happened yesterday, I've lost my taste for their company. But after last bell, they find me anyway, loitering by my locker, coming up on either side of my body and grabbing my elbows like a pair of *Sopranos* hit men.

"Come on," Eva giggles, flipping her hair. "No rehearsal today. We're kidnapping you."

"Boys' soccer on the upper field," Tori says in response to my bewildered look, turning and leading the way.

Resistance is futile. I follow them, crunching over leaves strewn across the field behind the school. We clamber up onto the chilly gunmetal bleachers, finding seats way at the top, putting our feet up on the bench below. The crowd is sparse; soccer has its groupies, mostly wannabe Anglophiles, but not enough to pack the stands like football or basketball. The players down on the field look like honeybees buzzing around a field of clover, decked out in our school's yellow-and-black colors.

"Amos!" Eva spots him and waves wildly to get his attention. He sees us, and turns. A flicker of something—displeasure? embarrassment?—flashes across his face. He quickly waves back, then heads into the throng of players. *Trouble in paradise?* I wonder, glancing over at Eva. But her face reveals nothing.

I absently half-listen while Eva and Tori start gossiping; Tori complains again about the travesty of an early gym class, Eva bashes Ms. Pinella for not giving her one more second to get through the last answer on the math test, and how hard was that bonus question?

But what does it all matter? In light of my dad's life crisis, my family's newfound status on the dole, it all strikes me as petty. Insignificant. Actually, I have to admit, compared to my nightly discussions with Annalise, everything Eva and Tori talk about seems pretty pointless.

"So, sale at LuLu's tomorrow," Eva says, mentioning the local boutique we all love. "Anyone want to check out the racks?"

Tori says she's in, but I hesitate, wondering if I am still allowed to go clothes shopping. Even with a sale, LuLu's is not cheap, and we'd already bought a bunch of back-to-school clothes before my dad's big announcement. I know my parents had told me we'd be fine, finance-wise, but after last night's fight, things have been über-tense at home. I hadn't thought through how my dad's decision left us on the brink of danger. Would we become like some of those people you heard about on the news—losing our house, drowning in debt, bankrupt? Homeless, even? Maybe my mom was right: He should have kept quiet and sucked it up. What would she say if she found out I'd been the one who planted the seed of encouragement in his mind? Would she blame me?

I say nothing, knowing what will happen if I share my financial fears. My friends would tsk ooohhh nooo, and give each other a *look* over my head, which meant they'd be texting frantically about me the minute I turned my back. Once my clothing budget is limited to Target, how long before Eva and Tori's trash talk turns on me?

"Maybe," I hedge, thinking of a way I could bring in some extra cash on my own. The math department is always looking for tutors, and Ms. Pinella is always asking if I am interested. There is that. Eva shrugs and moves on to gossiping about the school principal, who is rumored to wear a hairpiece to cover his bald spot. "What about a reverse pageant?" Eva asks Tori. "Worst-looking teacher at Dansville High!"

I watch as Eva gazes at Tori, seeking her reply. Her approval. Tori considers it for a moment, then regally shakes her head. "No way. I get enough drama without pissing off the entire faculty."

"I know," Eva clucks sympathetically. Then Eva snaps her fingers and turns to me. "Oh, before I forget. What excuse did you come up with for Declan's no-show yesterday?" She says it casually, like the drama we set in motion is no big deal.

I recap how I'd said his parents came home unexpectedly, and she nods in approval.

"So all is forgiven?"

"For now." I realize neither of them knows what happened afterwards, and explain how Annalise somehow bumped into Colin Dirge at the mall and he offered to leave her free tickets at the door.

"Un-be-liev-a-ble," Eva drawls when I finish the story, looking outraged. "That girl always gets her way. I wonder what she did for him—"

I don't bring up the fact that she herself waltzed off with a pair of front row tickets and a chance to perform on stage with the band, over the hundreds of way more devoted Knucklies. Cooper was right: people like Eva didn't seem to need luck. They make their own—through sheer force of will, if necessary.

Tori leans closer to me. "Seriously, Noelle, do you realize every single person we know is going to this concert but us? I downloaded that song and now I really like them." I know what she means. That band has a way of worming into your affections even if you try to resist. Sort of like Annalise herself.

"Speaking of fangirl, should we see what she's up to?" Eva says, whipping out her phone.

I am silent, as I watch her try repeatedly, locked out of the account until finally, she glances over at me, frustrated. "What's the deal, Noey? It keeps saying I have the wrong password. Did you change it or something?"

I feign sudden recall. "Um, oh yeah."

"Why?" she demands.

I want to tell her the real reason so badly it hurts. *Because I don't want you playing Annalise anymore.* But all my fearlessness from the night before escapes me now. So I backslide into a lie. "Oh, I, ah, forgot it, and I got locked out, so I had to reset it." I grab her phone and quickly type it in for her, so she can't see. Then I summon up my last ounce of nerve. "But I've been thinking, we have to be more consistent, Eva. We can't have one of us writing one thing and then the other writing something else later. What if she notices? We're going to get busted, don't you think?"

"I guess," she concedes.

Sensing my opening, I add quickly, "And since you guys have been so busy with play practice, and now your song, and Tori's got her pageant stuff, I'm fine with staying on top of it."

Eva stares at me, trying to read my face, slowly twirling a finger around a long strand of hair. "That's really sweet of you, Noey. Just, you know, we were talking at lunch—where were you, anyway? But listen, I get it. Tori was saying, chatting with her every night. It's only natural you might start sympathizing with her."

"Yeah," Tori adds. "It's like . . . whatchamacallit. When the bad guys slowly convince their hostage they're really not so bad?"

"Stockholm syndrome," Eva nods. "But her sweet act? It's not real. She thinks you're the love of her life. Of course, she's nice to you."

"I know," I try to protest.

Eva leans closer to me. "But we all know what she's really like. What she is capable of. Right? Just make sure you're don't forget that."

"I won't," I say, shaking my head, wondering if Eva is right, wondering if it's already happened. "But, honestly, you guys. She's not all bad."

They both don't answer me, giving one another a look. I know instantly I've said the wrong thing.

"Maybe Noelle *is* confused." Tori nods her head knowingly at Eva. "You know, like we said." They both smirk at each other.

"What?" A pause. "What?" I repeat, an edge of bile rising in my throat.

Eva looks at me with her lips still curled. "She means, maybe you're falling for her for real."

Then I catch on to the meaning of their words. And I can't believe it. Eva wouldn't really go there, would she? Tori might, but not my oldest friend. "I am not! You know I like Cooper that way. I'm doing this for Cooper."

My eyes plead with her and the silence drags on and on, until finally she says, "Kid-ding!" She and Tori suddenly jump up, clapping loudly and whooping, and I turn and see that Amos has just scored a goal.

Somehow, this is going all wrong. My dad had managed to stand up for himself, why can't I? I feel like I have wandered into quicksand, and any effort I make to fight it only sucks me in deeper. I read once that this is what it feels like to drown, that eventually, you just grow weak and give up, and the water blankets you into submission.

"Maybe you're right." I say, submitting to my fate, circling the drain.

Eva nods, gracious in victory. "Keep your eyes on the prize."

Still, I am the one on the hook, and need to know our end game. I remind her we can't keep this up forever. The story I used for Declan—about being grounded until his mom gets the cast off—was only going to give us a few more weeks.

"Right," Eva agrees, waving her hand dismissively. "So maybe, there's a complication. Her wrist never healed right and she needs two more weeks. You see?"

I say I do, but I'm not unconvinced. That eventually, I think Annalise will figure it out.

Eva just shakes her head, blithely unconcerned. "Nah. She'll keep believing because she *wants* to believe. We all do. As long as we don't tell her, we're fine. Like, what's she going to do? Show up on his doorstep in Worcester?"

CHAPTER 19

ANNALISE

Over the next few excruciating minutes, three things become extremely obvious: a) Maeve and Declan are super-delighted to see one another again because, b) Declan is also a longtime camper at Camp Chicawawa, and c) Maeve and Declan have completely forgotten all about me. They start swapping stories about fellow campers and beloved counselors and even subject the entire neighborhood to a quick rendition of some Color War-winning cheer, until eventually, they run out of good times to relive and notice I am still standing there, speechless.

"So, wait, what *are* you doing here?" Declan finally says to Maeve, who looks over at me.

She shakes her head delightedly at me, as if this is all some happy coincidence. "I can't believe your Declan from Worcester is Dec O'Keefe from Chicawawa!"

"*Her* Declan?" Declan repeats uncertainly, still looking at Maeve for answers, as I realize I'd never told her Declan's last name.

I kind of clear my throat until I have his attention, although I don't understand what is happening. Why did Declan recognize Maeve—but not me? Do I look that different in real life?

"It's me, Annalise," I say, lamely, trying to jar his recognition.

"I'm sorry," he says, peering at me more carefully now, but still with a look of polite confusion. "Do I know you?"

I'm completely floored. "Know me?" I croak out. "Are you kidding? We've only been chatting online every night."

"I'm sorry, you must have me confused with someone else," he says, glancing at Maeve for support. "I don't do online chatting."

The blood drains from my face. Is this a joke? Am I getting Punk'd? No, I get it, he must be covering up because his parents are hovering somewhere nearby, listening to us, and he wasn't supposed to be using the computer that way while he was grounded.

I lower my voice and talk urgently, sure this is it. "Declan, it's me. We met on the fan site? Brass Knuckles?"

But no.

It gets worse. He crinkles his nose. "Brass Knuckles?" he repeats as if I'm speaking in Swahili.

Frustrated, I pull out my phone and pull up his profile on the site. "Isn't this you?" I demand, pushing it into his palm. "Declan O'Keefe? Homeschooled. Live in Worcester?"

He stares at it for a long time, scrolling back through some of our conversations, then hands it back reluctantly. "That's my photo," he slowly admits. "But I never wrote any of that. And I still don't understand why you're here."

We stare angrily at each other. What am I supposed to say now? *I'm here because I like you?* I'm not even sure that I do. This guy is nothing like my Declan. He talks in this stiff, formal way, and his teeth are kind of off and he's scrawnier than he looked in his photo. And his eyes are cold, distrustful, foreign. Any attraction I might have had to Declan O'Keefe is rapidly fading now that I'm standing here in front of him in the flesh. Especially after hearing him tell Maeve about a million times how great she looks.

I glance at her for help, but she hesitates, unsure what to say. Why had she never mentioned Declan? Or had she? Maeve went on and on about her camp stories and of course, Aiden Sylvester, the Junior Olympic blond Adonis that was her summertime obsession, but I wasn't sure if she ever mentioned a dark, wiry guy named Dec.

Finally, Maeve attempts to explain things. "Annalise has been chatting online with someone who said he was Declan O'Keefe," she says. "We came to meet him—you—in person."

"Well, I'm not . . . whoever." He crosses his arms, as if that is the end of that.

My head is swimming, as a million questions pound in my brain. Is Declan putting me on, for some sick reason? Are we at the wrong house? Is it possible I have the wrong Declan O'Keefe, that there is another, unlisted O'Keefe family somewhere in Worcester? And if none of those possibilities is true, it begs the most important question: If *this* is the one and only Declan O'Keefe, and he has no idea who I am, then WHO ON EARTH have I been talking to all this time? Who has been filling my brain with their thoughts and opinions and insights, night after night after night?

"I think someone's been playing you," he finally says, stating the obvious.

"What? Like she's being catfished?" Maeve's face scrunches in concern. "Like that MTV show?"

Declan looks at her, confused, then shrugs. "I don't know. We don't get cable."

But I've seen the show and know exactly what she means. My mind reels as everything I thought was true dissolves like cotton candy in a rainstorm. "You mean, my Declan is a fake? But I must have been talking to someone. I didn't just imagine it. Who would do this?"

Maeve and Declan swap a glance of pity. My face is burning. I know what Maeve must be thinking: a big, fat I told you so. Why hadn't I listened to her? Why hadn't I ever asked for his home number, or suggested a video chat, before making this fool's pilgrimage to Worcester? Who hated me so much they would do this to me—and why?

"Forget it," I say to Declan, just wanting to get out of there, to escape this humiliation. "Let's go," I tell Maeve, glancing up at the sky, which is growing darker by the minute. "The train back to Dansville leaves in an hour." She hesitates, clearly feeling bad to leave Declan on such weird terms. "Are you coming?"

"Wait a sec." Declan reaches to touch my arm, stopping me. "You guys live in Dansville?"

"Yeah, why?" Maeve asks.

"Oh, probably nothing, just my cousin lives there. Eva?"

Slowly, I turn back around to face him. "Eva Winters?"

He nods.

Maeve has a look of horror on her face, and my brain is processing this news as fast as hers. "Does Eva have this picture of you?" I pull out my phone again and we all three examine the photo. This time, his face lights up in recognition. "Oh jeez, that was, yeah, that was taken at our family reunion this summer. I think she was next to me, but she must have been cropped out."

"Or cropped herself out," Maeve says dryly, pointing to the sliver of a bare leg, barely visible next to his, which I'd never noticed before.

Within minutes, the three of us have pieced it all together. Maeve tells Declan the backstory: what happened with Amos, why Eva tormented me last year and hates me to this day. Now I know why Eva insisted on being at the mall that day: to get a front row view of Declan standing me up. I more than obliged.

Declan shakes his head angrily, erasing any lingering suspicions I had that he was in on it with his cousin. "That's a rotten, dirty trick. Really vile."

I think I am going to be sick. It doesn't make sense. All this time—all these nights—I've been talking to Eva? It can't be. I mentally scroll through all the personal things I shared with her, potentially embarrassing things that now she can use against me. Being jealous of my sister. My dad's affair, how he left our family for Claire, how I couldn't forgive him. I'd confided all my weaknesses to my worst enemy.

"What do you want me to do?" Declan asks me. "Tell my parents? Or call her myself, tell her to knock it off?"

I mentally weigh my options, which range from sucks to totally blows.

Scenario A: Declan tells his parents, who'd tell Eva's parents, who'd get her busted. Maybe, depending upon whether they were the kind of parents who cared about that stuff. And she'd hate me ten times over. And she'd make sure the word got out at school that I was so desperate, I fell for some online boyfriend who didn't exist.

Scenario B: I tell my mom, who'd freak out and call the principal, who'd get Eva suspended or maybe even expelled, depending upon whether he was the kind of principal who cared about that stuff. And she'd hate me twenty times over. And she'd make sure the word got out at school that I was so pathetic, I fell for some online boyfriend who didn't exist.

Scenario C: Declan tells Eva he knows, which would let her know I know, which would rule out any possibility of revenge. And she could still make sure the word got out at school.

Suddenly, anger overwhelms me. Just like the five stages of grief we studied in health class, my emotions shift from denial to rage. I want to grab Eva by the throat and strangle the life out of her. How dare she play me like that? Why won't she just leave me alone? This time, I don't want to roll over and take it.

"No," I tell him, a plan already forming in my mind. Maybe, I can take control. Turn the tables on Eva. "I'll handle it. For now, don't do a thing."

***

We ride home in silence. Maeve probably doesn't know exactly what to say, and I sit and stew, replaying every conversation over again in my mind, trying to put a face to the words, a rhyme to the reason. Maeve's phone bursts into song, breaking the awkwardness, and she gratefully answers it. "What? Yeah. Yeah. What?"

She listens, and through the phone's speakers I can hear someone's voice in the background, extremely upset. "Calm down." She sees me eyeing her in concern and mouths the name, Samantha. Her little sister. "Uh-huh. Uh-huh. You did what? Didn't I tell you—? You are not! No, Sam. I swear."

This goes on for a full ten minutes until she finally gets off the phone. She takes a deep breath and turns to me. Her face is purple with fury.

"What happened?" I ask, almost too scared to know. "Is everything okay?"

"Well, no one died," she says with a harsh laugh. "But no. Definitely not okay."

Apparently, Samantha had gone and entered Tori's weekly beauty pageant, against our express warnings. "She only got two votes," Maeve explains, "and some loser wrote U.G.L.Y. below her picture, and now she's devastated. Saying she wants a nose job. I mean, I seriously can't believe someone would be so low as to insult a little girl like that. It's sick!"

"That's so messed up!" I can't believe someone would slam sweet, beautiful little Samantha, although a small, less generous, part of me wonders why her sister—or any girl, really—had to be such an attention-seeker and enter these contests in the first place. And then I immediately feel evil for thinking that, like an eleven-year-old kid should know any better. But still.

Maeve grabs my hand and squeezes it tightly. "Whatever you're planning to do to get back at Eva and her friends. I'm in. I am so, so in."

CHAPTER 20
NOELLE

On Saturday morning, I wake to the smell of chocolate chip pancakes, luring me out of my bed and down the stairs. As I pass by my dad's office, I hear his voice inside, talking to someone, this serious tone in his voice. I slow down to try to figure out who he's talking to and catch the phrase, "going solo."

Going solo? I linger, trying to hear a little more, but suddenly the door swings open, nearly banging into me. "Oh, hi honey," Dad says, emerging and carefully shutting the door behind him.

"Who were you calling?" I ask.

He pauses, then answers me. "Pro shop. Making a tee-time."

I relax. What was I thinking, anyway? Going solo obviously means he's playing golf as a single.

"Any plans today?" he asks, and I shrug, following him as he heads down the hall.

In the kitchen, my mom is sitting at the counter, sipping some home-brewed Starbucks and reading the *Boston Globe*, my parents' normal morning routine. Only she is doing it all alone.

"I'm heading out," he tells her curtly, grabbing his keys and his rain jacket.

"Fine," she replies just as coolly. I can tell what she's thinking. That he should be spending every waking moment scouring the job boards. Meanwhile, my dad would say he does his best thinking—and networking—out on the links.

"I'm playing with Bob Pontin," he tells her pointedly. "He may have some leads for me."

"Great," she says through gritted teeth.

Now I am confused. If my dad is playing with Bob Pontin, then why is he *going solo*?

Before I can crack that mystery, my cell phone buzzes. It's Eva, wanting me to meet her and Tori at LuLu's at 11:00. She always says that I can calculate 40 percent off a $59.99 skirt faster than she can whip out her mom's AmEx. But I'm starting to dread the thought of being around her, waiting for her next scheme to slam Annalise. Or me.

The phone buzzes again, demanding a reply. When I push decline, my mom gets all nosy.

"Aren't you going to get that?" she asks.

"They're going shopping at LuLu's," I croak, my mouth dry and teeth still unbrushed.

"Don't you want to go?" she asks. "You should go."

I hesitate. "I'm not really in the mood," I finally say. "I think I'll go swimming instead." Even though swim season doesn't officially start until winter, I still go a few times a week to stay toned.

My mom spots an opportunity. "Well, if you want to take a break, I could use your help. The winter line is in, and I brought home some last-minute product I need to sort before Monday's photo shoot. Maybe you could help when you get back?"

"Sure," I say, hiding my lack of enthusiasm. My mom's always trying to push her company's product on me, insisting this eyeliner or that lip gloss would "enhance" my natural looks. Meaning, make me look less plain vanilla, more Chai Spice. But every time I put that goop on my face, I immediately want to dive in the pool and wash it all away.

I'm about to head back upstairs, but something compels me into my dad's office instead. I slip inside and stop by his desk, where I notice a notepad lying on top with his unintelligible handwriting scribbled all over it. Beside it, there's a business card from the law firm of Haddock, Nelson, & Pike. I'm starting to get freaked out. Going solo? Lawyers? Lying about golf partners. What does this mean? Why would he even be talking to an attorney? Is it possible that my dad is thinking about . . . about getting a divorce?

I wonder what Annalise would think. She's the only friend I can think of who's just been through this with her own parents. Even though it was an affair that broke them up, maybe she'd still recognize the warning signs. How to know when things are really getting bad. Bad enough to worry. I try messaging Annalise as Declan, but she doesn't respond. Where is she? I really want to talk to her. *Need* to talk to her. Come to think of it, I haven't heard from her at all since the day before yesterday. What's going on?

I decide the best way to distract myself is to head over to the pool. I change into my bathing suit and grab my gym bag with goggles and towel and flip flops. "I'm heading out," I call to my mom, slipping out the door before she can answer. I bike the few blocks down to the local Y, enjoying the blue sky, the crisp fall day.

When I get there, the place is empty, just the way I like it. Only one of the pool's six lap lanes is occupied. Everyone must be out picking apples or enjoying one last beach day or a hike in the woods before the arctic winter sets in. Their loss. I dive into the cool water, kicking hard, wishing I could leave my troubles in my wake. Gliding below the surface always clears my head. Sometimes, it feels like the only place I can see things clearly. I hold my breath and stay underwater as long as I possibly can.

***

When I get home, I find my mom in the dining room, surrounded by stacks of cardboard boxes. She pleads for me to stay and help her. "Come on," she says. "You used to love doing this."

Yeah, I reply in my head. *When I was, like, six.* "Fine," I sigh, even though I am on to her. She thinks this forced mother-daughter bonding time will get me to reveal my inner angst. Well, Mom, think again. We start opening different packages and sort the makeup into piles all along the mahogany table: mascara wands, lip liners, brushes, compacts, and gels.

"Do you want to try this?" she asks, holding up a sparkly purple eyeliner. I take it, inspecting it before I wrinkle my nose. "A little too Lady Gaga." I hold up the eyeliner. "But can I give it to Tori?"

"Sure."

"Great." Maybe if I keep bribing her with swag, I will be safe from her wrath. I pocket a few extra tubes of shimmery body lotion, too, just to be sure.

"So how are Eva and Tori?" I grimace at hearing the names, but try to hide it.

"Oh, that reminds me. There's something Tori wanted me to ask you." I tell my mom about Tori's crazy idea that her company should sponsor her online beauty pageant and mention products in return for giveaways to *InstaHotOrNot* contestants.

"Hmm." My mom's face is busy scrutinizing some label, making her reaction unclear.

"It's dumb, I know." I backpedal, already sorry I asked.

She raises her head and looks at me. "No, that's very entrepreneurial of her. Tell her to write me a proposal. I'll pass it around to the right people."

"Wait, really?" I guess I fail to hide the disdain on my face because my mother fixes her dark brown eyes on me.

"Yes, why not? I know you think this is just a bunch of makeup," she says, waving at the boxes at our feet. "But this is a real industry, a real profession, and besides all that, it happens to pay our bills. And, yes I use makeup and Botox. The reality is, the working world judges you on your looks. I'm in a youth business, and I have to keep my edge."

"I know that," I tell her. Up close, I can see my mother's laugh lines around her mouth and tiny crow's feet by her eyes. Is my mother worried about losing her job, too? What if that happens? Or is she worrying about something else? The Big D?

I finally work up the nerve to ask in a roundabout way what I've been wondering all day. "Is everything okay around here?"

"What?" If she is at all caught off guard by my question, she quickly recovers. "Yes. Of course. We're going to be fine. Not heading to the poor house. Yet." She purses the corner of her lips, to let me know this is just a joke. "Wait. Is that why you didn't want to go with your friends today?"

I hesitate. It isn't, but it's easier to let her think that, so I kind of shrug again, like it might be. "Just because your dad's not working, you can still go shopping. Don't go crazy or anything—" She breaks off and leans towards me. "You know, honey, I'll tell you a little secret. I actually make more money than your dad ever has."

This is news to me. "You do?"

"Yup. Unlike your friends' moms, who've been busy taking yoga classes all these years." I know she's making a dig at Eva's mom, who is part of this exercise-obsessed clique that Eva calls "the tiny hineys." She nods with satisfaction. "Well, luckily for us, I've kept working." I think back to elementary school, when all the other moms were room mothers and field trip chaperones, and mine was always too busy at the office. But now, they all thought her job was super cool, especially Tori, who was horrified and swore us all to secrecy when her mom took a part-time holiday job folding scarves at Chico's.

She gazes at me steadily. "A woman should never completely depend on someone else. She should be able to stand on her own two feet. Be prepared for the worst. That's what I've always believed. That's what Nana and Papa wanted for me, and that's what I want for you, too. Don't you agree?"

"Sure."

As mottos go, it's not the worst I've ever heard. I wish I had enough courage to stand on my own, instead of clinging to a sinking friendship. But inside, my spirits droop. *Stand on her own two feet? Never depend on another? Prepare for the worst?* It sounds like my fears could be right. My mom and dad's marriage is definitely on the rocks.

CHAPTER 21

ANNALISE

Bam. Bam. Bam. I'm running through a Plexiglass funhouse maze, trying to find Declan. But no matter which way I turn, I ram into something cold, glassy, hard. *Bam*. With a gasp I wake up to the ringing of the house phone. For a blissful moment, I don't remember any of what went down the day before, and then my stomach sours and it all comes rushing back. Worcester. Declan. Catfishing. Humiliation.

I groan and stumble down to the kitchen, fumbling to find the handset, to see who on god's green earth would be calling us so early on a Saturday morning. On the land line, no less.

It's Elena. "Where's mom?" my sister demands, not bothering with a polite hello or to ask how I am.

"Hello to you, too," I croak, still strangely comforted to hear her voice. Part of me wonders if I should confide in her, if maybe she might even have some good advice on what to do about the whole DecOlan-Eva disaster. Despite our rocky relationship, we've shared some rare moments of sister solidarity.

"Hello, hello," she says impatiently. "Is she there? I tried her on her cell, like, three times and she's not picking up."

I rack my brain, trying to remember what my mom had told me sometime way early this morning, when she'd poked her head into my room and said she'd be back later in the day. I'd been half asleep, still trying to block out the cruel world.

"No, she's out," I tell Elena. "Having brunch with a friend in the city."

"Who? Diane?" Diane was my mom's only good friend in Boston, a Back Bay realtor she'd roomed with in college.

"Dunno," I shrug. She had only said something about brunch before she dashed out of the house.

"Well, I need to talk to her about Head of the Charles," Elena says importantly.

"You're rowing?" I ask, somewhat surprised.

Head of the Charles is this super prestigious regatta for the top crew teams held every fall on the Charles River in Cambridge, near Harvard Square. When we were little, when my parents still enjoyed doing things together, they used to take us down to cheer on the boats, and I guess that's when Elena caught the bug to become a rower.

"Yeah, in the frosh boat. You guys are coming, right?"

"I guess," I say. "When is it?"

She tells me the date and I make a mental note of it. "Well, Mom's been spacey lately. You better make sure she puts it in her calendar."

"What, you mean because of your dumb tickets?" Elena says. "Yeah, she told me. That's not spacey, Lise, she got in a car accident."

"No, I don't mean the tickets," I reply, annoyed. Clearly, she hasn't heard the good news that I'm getting tickets from Colin Dirge, and there's no way, now, I'm telling her the whole convoluted story of why I was running crying through the mall in the first place.

"Then what?" I can tell she doesn't believe me. Our mom has always been the most organized person I know, with lists and schedules and routines.

"I don't know, just forgetting little stuff."

"You don't think she's sick, or something?" Elena asks, her voice rising in alarm, which makes me feel slightly better. I was wondering the same thing, and it would have been so typical of my mom to confide in my big sister but not me. They both still treat me like the baby in the family, even though I'm only an inch shorter than Elena. But if she didn't know anything, then maybe there really was nothing to know.

"I don't know. She hasn't said anything to you?"

"Nope. She's probably fine, Lise," she says in that annoying big-sister tone of hers. "She's probably just, you know, menopausal or something. Dad didn't say anything."

I can't help but snort. "Like he would know." Dad doesn't have a clue about Mom's life anymore. She's in the past. His ex. Would he even care if there was something wrong with her? With me?

"Well, he didn't," Elena insists.

"So you talked to him?"

"Yeah," she says casually. "The other day." I just don't get how Elena can still have this super close relationship with my dad, after everything that happened. Our conversations, even this summer, always feel so forced. "You should call him."

"Why? Did he say something?"

"Just that he hasn't heard from you in over a week. You shouldn't blow him off. Look, I just said I'd remind you. Don't kill the messenger, okay?"

Easy for her to say. She had to skip out on our annual August visit this year, since it conflicted with her freshman orientation, leaving me spending three awkward weeks with him, Claire, and the twins, all on my own. A fact I now remind her of. "I think I've had enough quality family time for one lifetime."

"He just wants to see how school's going. That's what we talked about. He's bummed he can't make it up here for the race. Oh, and he said he was sending me something."

"Just you?" I can't help ask, jealous again that she is always the favored one.

"I don't know, Lise. I'm sure you, too," she assures me.

I half snort in disbelief.

"Why do you have to be so hard on him?" Elena asks.

"Why do you always let him off so easy?" I shoot back. Why didn't Elena have as hard a time getting over Dad's betrayal as I did? Was it because she loved him more? Or less?

Her voice softens. "Look, Lise. I know the whole thing sucks."

I concede her point with silence. The phone line crackles as we listen to each other breathing. I wish I could be as forgiving as Elena, but I don't know if I can. Most of all, I wish Elena hadn't bailed on me this summer when I needed her to be there.

"Elena?" I finally ask, my voice growing soft, too.

"What?"

"How can you just forgive him?"

She pauses for a long moment. "Because he got swept up in something he wasn't strong enough to stop. He was weak, I know. But also I know he didn't want to hurt us. Can't you, you know, give him another chance? Maybe he'll surprise you."

I think about that but don't have a reply.

"So how is it, up there?" I ask, changing the subject, wishing I could get out of the next three years of high school early and join her. When I wander into her room now, it's weird how it's been stripped bare, how all her photos and trinkets have been reassembled somewhere else, in a dorm room miles away.

"Amazing." And she goes on and on about late night Dominos with her dorm mates, and this frat party she went to where everyone dressed as angels or devils, and her Intro to Psych course where they get to be human lab rats, until finally, she remembers to play the part of Concerned Older Sister and ask about my life back at Dansville High. "So, how is Dullsville?"

I tell her about math with Pinella, whom she had sophomore year, too, and Maeve making the volleyball team. "How about those witches from last year—they're not still trash-talking you, are they?" One night, early in the summer, Elena had forced the story out of me after rumors of the Freshman Fling melodrama somehow trickled up into the senior stratosphere.

But the urge to confide in my sister is somehow gone, the moment passed.

"No," I lie, since technically they've moved on to way more sophisticated forms of torture. "It's pretty much the same old, same old."

CHAPTER 22

NOELLE

I hope Eva realizes we are going to hell, or if not hell, at least, a state penitentiary.

At church this morning, Pastor Reilly's entire sermon thundered against the sin of lying.

"Who among us has ever deceived another? Dissembled? Lied? Prevaricated? Told untruths?"

Me, me, me, me and, oh yeah, me.

The whole time, I was sure he was looking right at me, knowing that practically everything I'd said to Annalise online was based on a lie, and that even if God forgave me for it, she probably wouldn't.

Besides, it wasn't just the higher power I needed to worry about smiting me down. I'd typed in the words "Internet" and "impersonation" and "false" into Google last night and discovered that what we'd done was breaking the law in a whole bunch of states and could cost us tons of money in fines—or even land us in jail. The main legal distinction was whether we'd done it as a prank or "maliciously" to cause "emotional distress." I think again of Annalise, running through the mall in tears, and am positive we're going to end up in a jail cell. The legal fees alone will bankrupt the little money my parents have left after they split their assets. I forwarded the link to Eva, who texted me back to quit worrying, saying that prison chic was so in, hadn't I heard that orange is the new black?

As we all file out into the banquet hall for post-sermon coffee, Cooper and his parents come over to greet my family. Our dads shake hands casually, while our moms air kiss and exchange pleasantries.

"How are you?" I hear Cooper's mom ask mine, scanning her face, as if she knows the answer is written there.

I wish Mom would tell the truth: *My husband's out of work and considering divorce, my Botox bankroll is running low, and my daughter's close to being busted for online fraud. How 'bout you?*

"Great, just fine," my mom chirps, negating the sermon we'd just listened to five minutes ago—although she does shoot me a look when I roll my eyes and audibly cough in disbelief.

"Why don't you and Cooper go get some cake?" she suggests.

Cooper looks agreeably at me and I nod. The two of us duck over to the dessert table, where we always stuff our napkins with whatever baked goods the sisterhood has provided that week, then head out to the courtyard to scarf them down. The fall air is growing crisp, but still warm so long as you stand in the sun. I love being privy to Cooper's church persona: a proper button-down shirt and shiny shoes, his hair damp and combed neatly, completely different from the bed head and T-shirt school version.

We lean against the low brick wall and I dig into my coffee cake, getting crumbs all over my black woolen skirt. I brush them off angrily. Too angrily. Cooper notices.

"What's up with you and your mom?"

Uncharacteristically, I find myself blurting out the truth. "I can't stand when she's so fake. Like, we could have our house burn down and be standing here in our underwear, and my mom would say, 'Oh, we're doing grrrreat, how about you?'

Cooper nods like he understands. "Moms can be crazy like that. Remember, like, in fifth grade, when we went away to Argentina for a whole week to visit relatives?"

"Vaguely."

He shakes his head. "Wasn't true. Me and my brother got lice, and she couldn't handle the shame of people knowing. We had to stay inside all week while she de-loused our scalps and disinfected the house. Every other kid just came back to school the next day with a shaved head, but not us."

"Seriously?"

He makes the Boy Scout three-finger salute. "True story. You're the only one I've ever told." He rolls his eyes heavenward. "Ah, the relief. I've been carrying it around all these years."

I laugh, feeling a little bit better. For some reason, with Cooper, I'm never shy, like I am with other boys at school. Maybe because I've known him my whole life, practically. I wonder for the billionth time if this great rapport is just all in my head. If not, then why doesn't he feel it, too? Is Tori right? Is it because I fail in the figure department? Does it really come down to stupid cup size—even for Cooper?

"So, what's the horrid truth she's covering up?" he asks, leaning in. "It's not good to keep it bottled up inside."

I hesitate although I know I can trust him. "Come on." He smiles encouragingly. "You tell me yours and I'll tell you mine."

What secrets could Cooper possibly have? Intrigued, I look around, making sure no one is near enough to overhear. Then in a rush, I tell him. "My dad quit his job. And my mom is pissed at him. She doesn't want anyone to know he's unemployed. Says it's our personal business. And I'm worried that all the stress might make them split up. They've been having huge fights over it."

He is right. For a moment, it does feel good to let my secret escape, to watch it float away, like a helium balloon carelessly slipping from a child's hand at a fair.

"Whoa. Out-of-work dad and fighting parents? Really dredging up some skeletons in the closet, there?" Cooper smiles kindly at me. "I thought you were going to tell me some real family scandal. A paternity suit, forged documents, traceless poisons, that kind of thing. That's all you got?"

He gazes at me, and for a moment, it feels like he is waiting for me to say something else. Something more. If only I had Eva's bravado, I would just spit it out. What had she said to do? Just make a move on him already. I want to open my mouth and scream, *No. That's not all. I am madly in love with you, you idiot!*

Instead, a sigh escapes my lips. "That's all." Isn't it enough? There's no way I can tell him the other secret hanging over my head, the complicated cat-and-mouse game I've got going with Annalise.

"Don't stress," he says. "I'm sure they're not going to divorce in the middle of all that. That doesn't make sense. Once he lands a new job, things will go back to normal. You'll see."

"Maybe," I concede, not convinced, but appreciating his attempt to cheer me up. "Now you." I am not hopeful. There is only one confession I want to hear from his lips, and I doubt I will ever get it.

"Me?" He waves his hands innocently in the air. "I got nothing. I just said that to make you go first."

"Cooper!" I playfully kick the pebbles on the ground toward him, sending a cloud of dirt onto his shiny brown shoes.

"Hey!" He feigns a coughing fit until the dust settles. "Okay, fine. It's no secret, probably. The whole darn school knows."

"Who you're into?" I say haltingly.

He nods in assent, frowning, as if remembering something. "I know you and your little crew aren't her big fans."

I ask if he heard what happened last year, not sure how plugged in he is to the Dansville High rumor mill.

"Vaguely. Something that got Eva's knickers in a twist." Cooper shrugs. "I'd say that's a mark in her favor."

Cooper's never bothered to hide his dislike of Eva. He'd tried one time to get me to explain why I stayed friends with her, until I finally told him to drop it. He just doesn't get it, how high school is like a jungle: separate yourself from your pack, and you might be eaten alive.

"But I can't seem to figure her out," he continues. "She keeps sending me mixed signals. Hot and cold, you know? What do you think?"

I wish I could be anywhere else but here, having this conversation, but against my better judgment, I try to help. "For starters," I suggest, "try not insulting the band she's obsessed with."

He nods his head. "Yeah, I really put my foot in it there. Dumb, dumb. Why is my mouth like ten times ahead of my brain?"

I shrug, thinking I have the exact reverse problem.

"Maybe it's a lost cause. She turned down my offer to study. Said she was meeting that other guy at the mall."

Without thinking, I inform him that the guy never came.

"What?" He looks startled, happy, like a death-row prisoner who has been granted a last-minute reprieve. "Really? The dude never showed?"

"Nope," I say, regretting I have opened my mouth. "She was pretty bummed. And then Eva won those tickets she wanted."

He nods. "I heard about that." Not surprising. You'd have to be under a rock; Tori had been blasting the news out incessantly over her feed to the entire population of Dansville High.

"Yeah. She was devastated. She practically begged Eva to take her, like Eva would ever—"

Cooper's face gets a visible tic, like something in his brain has clicked into place.

He pushes himself off the wall, little white crumbs flying off his pants and onto the grass below. "No, you're a genius! That's it."

"Cooper!" His dad materializes at the doorway to the courtyard, gesturing to him that it's time to go. "Coming," he says, patting me on one arm, like I am a favored pet. "Later!" Then he dashes back inside before I can figure out exactly what fresh damage I have done.

CHAPTER 23

ANNALISE

All weekend, "DecOlan" has been desperately trying to reach me, and by Sunday night, I am finally ready to respond. I let him find me online, live tweeting the Teen Pick Music Awards with all the other Knucklies, waiting for Brass Knuckles to take home the best new rock band award.

DecOlan: where have u been?

KnuckLise99: sorry. tied up w/family.

KnuckLise99: <<grrr>> u won't believe this.

DecOlan: what?

KnuckLise99: remember that creep i told u about?

DecOlan: y. why?

KnuckLise99: he hit on me at Tedeschi's yesterday.

KnuckLise99: <<slimebag alert>> asked if I wanted to hook up sometime!!

DecOlan: he did not!?

KnuckLise99: yeah! i was all like, don't you have a girlfriend? and he was like, she doesn't have to know . . . gross!

It's all a lie, of course. It's part of the plan Maeve and I have dubbed Operation Payback, to get back at Eva over her little catfishing scheme. After brainstorming tons of ideas, we decided to hit Eva where it would hurt her the most: her heart.

That is, if she even has one.

DecOlan: what did you say?

KnuckLise99: bug off. obviously. what a loser.

KnuckLise99: I hear I'm not the only one he's tried . . . even hooked up with her airhead best friend. his gf has no idea. Sad.

It was Maeve's insistence that we find a way to involve Tori, as well. On the train ride home from Worcester, Maeve had texted Tori, asking her to take the mean posts about Samantha down, but Tori'd replied that she can't "be responsible" for the comments section. That she doesn't "condone censorship" of her audience and supports the "First Amendment." "Like she'd even know what the Constitution was if it bit her in the ass!" Maeve had ranted. "She probably thinks it's the freakin' boat in the Navy Yard." The best part of our plan was, if it worked, it would turn Eva and Tori against each other, ripping up their evil coven for good.

It's obvious, from the way that "DecOlan" (a.k.a. Eva) makes some bogus excuse and logs off lightning fast, that our story has hit home. By tomorrow morning at school, I'm hoping to see a full-blown nuclear meltdown go off before first bell, but I'll settle for a long, drawn-out whisper campaign as well. Of course, Amos and Tori will deny it, but there's no way Eva will forgive an indiscretion, not a second time, not with a close friend. I do feel a little bad that the poor guy has no idea what is in store for him, but I force any trace of sympathy from my brain. He's just as guilty as she is for what happened, right? He played me, then let everyone believe all those stories, without speaking up to say they weren't true.

HOW EVA REACTS:

Scenario A: Eva goes off on Amos in the cafeteria in front of everyone, dumping a tray of chicken noodle soup over his head before she proceeds to dump his sorry ass.

Scenario B: Eva and Tori get in a nasty catfight before they are broken up by Mr. Vange, the security guard.

Scenario C: I find Amos curled up in the fetal position, alone and crying, in a stairwell. But this time, instead of stopping to ask if he's okay, I stomp right on his toes, ruining his varsity soccer career just like he stomped all over my reputation.

Scenario D: Ideally, all of the above.

***

Monday morning, I scan the benches where their clique usually sits before school. I see a few of their crew: Tess McDonohue, Amanda Gerard. But no Eva. No Tori. No Amos. Is this a sign that it's already starting? Maybe all three are having it out somewhere in private. But where?

My stomach spasms into overdrive as I spot Amos, ambling across the quad with a group of friends. But no, it's not him, just his freshman doppelganger.

I exhale as Maeve shows up, a mad gleam in her eye. "Anything yet?"

"Nothing."

"Chill out. They'll show."

I nod.

"So . . ." Maeve says a little too casually. "You'll never guess who called me last night."

"Who?" I am still distracted, peering around the courtyard for Eva, Amos, and Tori.

"Dec. The real one."

"Oh?" I wait for her point. "What did he want?"

"To discuss our plan to kidnap the Kardashian kid. What do you think? Catch up on more camp gossip, I guess."

"Huh."

"Actually, he mentioned maybe us getting together sometime," she says, deliberately looking down at her ginormous feet. "If that's okay with you."

I think back on the boy in the flesh, the stiff, condescending boy whose onscreen face I had gazed at romantically so many nights. Face-to-face, I had to admit there was no chemistry. Zip. Nada. Still, I feel a twinge of betrayal that I try to rise above. "Look, you don't have ask my permission. Go out with him if you want."

"Oh please," she says, and in the way she flushes when she says it, I can tell she doesn't mean it at all. "I wouldn't. He's kind of a dork, you know? Not really my type."

"Okay, then."

She pauses for a beat. "Unless you *really* don't care either way."

"I don't." Why shouldn't Maeve have Declan, even if technically he was mine, sort of?

"I mean, it might be fun for old time's sake."

I try to nod agreeably, but the more she tries to convince me, the more ticked off I become. "Anyway, I've known him way longer than you." Like that gives her some claim on him?

Finally, I explode.

"What's that supposed to mean?"

She holds up her hands innocently. "Nothing. It's just that you never were really talking to him, you know? It's just a bizarre coincidence that I bumped into him that way. It's too bad, if you'd shown me his picture or told me his last name, we would have figured it out. Avoided all this grief."

Here it was, finally. I knew she'd never let me get away without the obligatory I-told-you-so. The I-knew-it-all-along. "What are you saying? That this is my fault?"

"Well, I knew something seemed fishy. All those stories. Being grounded. No phone to text. Bailing at the mall. New to social media. It didn't add up."

"Nice to blame the victim," I say in a huff. "Like maybe your sister wouldn't have gotten her feelings hurt if she hadn't put herself up for display on a stupid online beauty pageant."

"That's different," she shoots back angrily. "But if you really want to go there, none of this would have happened if you hadn't pissed off Eva by going into the stairwell with her stupid boyfriend in the first place."

She blinks, like she knows she has gone too far, while I wince, stung by her words. I can't believe she would say that, when she of all people knows the whole story.

"Do what you want with Declan," I snap, rising to my feet. "Maybe you'd rather hang with him tomorrow night than go to the concert with me."

"Annalise," she pleads from behind me. "Wait. That's not what I meant. Don't be like that."

But I am already gone.

CHAPTER 24

NOELLE

Annalise's story floored me. Could it be true? Had Amos really hit on her this weekend? And other girls? Her airhead friend? Tori? And Eva had no idea? But why would Annalise say so otherwise? She has no reason to lie to Declan, who presumably doesn't know any of these people.

My head's been throbbing ever since I read those words, and now I'm here in math and I'm still not sure what to do. Tell Eva? Eva is still one of my best friends. Annalise is . . . I don't know what. I don't even know if I should be taking her word for it. What if Annalise had gotten it wrong? Misinterpreted the whole thing? Maybe she'd flirted with Amos again and he'd responded. Or maybe he was just playing her? Or maybe she was trying to get Declan jealous, testing his interest after he failed to show that day.

There's no way I can confide in Tori again if it's true. No, there's only one thing to do before I go and spill everything to Eva and risk her killing the messenger. One person to approach, although I can't imagine how.

I have to talk to Amos. Alone.

"Noelle!" Ms. Pinella breaks into my thoughts. She is standing right in front of me, holding out my math test from Friday.

"Sorry?"

"I said," she repeats, although not irritably for some reason, "that out of the entire class, only one of you got my bonus question right. You, Noelle."

Me? I'm not sure how I pulled that one off without studying. I silently thank my dad for blessing me with his genius math genes.

Then she lobs a grenade straight into my lap. "Would you please come up to the board and show the class how you calculated the correct answer?" She says it like it is a casual request. Like you'd ask someone to remove her hat or take a seat.

Every head swivels my way expectantly, or at least, it feels that way. I look at her, hoping she'll read the dread on my face, but she is nodding encouragingly and gesturing for me to go up to the board. There is no getting out of this. I slowly drag myself out of my chair, trying to not feel my ears burning. My breath has become shallow and my heart rate has accelerated, as if I'm about to go cliff diving in Acapulco, instead of walking ten steps to the front of the room.

I get to the white board and grab the Sharpie tightly. It's a rappel line, the only thing standing between me and a 10,000-foot plunge into a ravine.

I want to stay this way forever, facing the board, but one more second and everyone will start to murmur. So I slowly swivel and brave my classmates. They are looking, for the most part, completely uninterested in how I solved the problem. Except, maybe, for valedictorian-bound Min Lee, my sole mathlete competition, who looks annoyed that she has been upstaged. Eva is studiously doodling in her notebook, avoiding eye contact, like my dorkitude reflects badly on her. I don't dare look directly in Cooper's direction, but I can tell from the corner of my eye he is gazing at me encouragingly, waiting to hear me speak.

Imagine your audience naked, those Toastmasters gurus always say—but how can I, when it feels like I'm the one stripped bare?

My body feels totally exposed, every imperfection on display, from a scuff on my shoe to a flyaway hair. My voice, my posture, my articulation, all up for judgment. The whole room seems to be waiting for me to blow it, to stutter or freeze or say too many ums. Or worse, commit some social faux pas that will ricochet around the school and stick—like Tammy Henderson's unexpected period in white pants, which people will probably still be bringing up at our ten-year reunion.

"Go ahead." Ms. Pinella nods, no help at all, no acknowledgment that she has just ruined my day, my week, possibly my life. I feel pools of sweat beading on my forehead and inside my shirt. A familiar tune seizes my brain. *Fiiiiive gol-den rings.*

"Well, I took the probability . . ." I whisper, my throat clenching up. What if I have a seizure? A panic attack? An allergic reaction? If I faint dead away, can I get out of this?

"Lou-der," Tyler Walters calls, just to be an ass. A few kids titter. I hate this. I *hate* this.

I start again, a decibel louder this time, trying to remind myself that really, no one in the class cares what I say—unless I say something moronic. Better to just get it over with. "I took the probability . . ." As quickly as possible, I walk the class through my thinking and how I'd arrived at the correct answer.

I look over and see Cooper murmuring something into Annalise's ear. She nods. Ugh. I totally lose my train of thought. Where was I? *Fiiiiive gol-den rings.*

I stammer and Tyler and a few of the guys in the back snicker again. I can feel my ears turn flamingo pink. Instead of shooting him a dirty look, like she always does, Eva is just sitting there, her face a blank slate. Like she doesn't even know me. This time, for the first time, protection is not coming. My white knight has left the building.

So here's what it would be like, I realize. Standing on my own two feet. Completely exposed. Life in a post-Eva universe. I am like a deer separated from her herd on the savannah, the predators circling, smelling the whiff of fear.

Noelling. Noey. The nobody.

"And the odds ratio?" Ms. Pinella prompts me as I falter.

"Um, right." I plow through the last part of the problem, talking as fast as I can and probably not illuminating anything for anyone. But eventually I am finished and can slink back to my seat.

"Thank you, Noelle," Ms. Pinella says. "Nice job." I faintly hear Tyler and his buddies mimicking Ms. Pinella under their breath. I have survived for now. But only barely. I try to catch Eva's eye, but she is leaning over and whispering something to Amanda Gerard. And Annalise? She is staring down at her own test paper, like the answers there reveal the meaning of life.

As soon as the bell rings, I rush out of the room towards the girls' bathroom to try to repair the damage done—the sweat stains of fear, my matted bangs, my bruised psyche.

It takes ten more minutes until my heart rate returns to normal.

CHAPTER 25

ANNALISE

Could this day get any worse? First, my argument with Maeve this morning. Stupid, stupid, stupid. Then, no sign of Eva and Amos fighting at all. No whispers in the hall, no rumors being swapped between classes. Eva swaggered into math class a minute ago like nothing happened, no signs of a big fight with Amos or Tori, no tear-streaked mascara stains trailing down her cheeks. The girl is a pretty good actress, but even she couldn't cover up her emotions that well.

And now this.

A 66 on my math test.

"Come see me after class," Ms. Pinella has scrawled at the top of my page. This cannot be happening. There's no way my mom will let me go to a concert tomorrow night if I come home with this kind of grade. I am trying to figure out how I'm going to keep this from her when Cooper leans over and whispers he wants to talk to me after class, too.

I'm suddenly the most popular person in Room 209.

Noelle Spiers is standing at the board, explaining in fast-talk how she got the bonus question right, like the rest of us can possibly keep up with her superior brain, while all I can do is stare at the practically failing grade, feeling a sinking sensation in my stomach. I knew it would be bad, but not stay-after-class bad.

When the bell rings, I expect to see Cooper waiting for me, but instead, he bolts out of class, completely forgetting whatever it was he had to say. I brush away a twinge of . . . could it actually be *disappointment*? For what, Cooper? Another unreliable member of the male species? Whatever. Probably he wanted to study together again and changed his mind when he saw my abysmal test score. I slowly stuff my books in my bag, waiting for everyone to leave so I can go do the Walk of Shame over to Ms. Pinella's desk without the whole class knowing.

"Annalise." Ms. Pinella pulls her reading glasses off and lets them hang on a chain around her neck. She cocks her head at me in concern. "What happened? Do you not understand the material? You seemed to be doing okay so far. Or were you having an off day?"

"Yeah, that," I mumble, not needing to tell her that instead of studying, I'd spent the afternoon before the test reenacting a Shakespearean melodrama down at the mall. "A really off day."

She looks at me quizzically. "Everything okay?"

"Yes," I nod. "Now it is."

She sighs. "Well, in my book everyone is entitled to one mulligan."

Mulligan?

"Golf term," she says, smiling at my puzzled expression. "It means a do-over. So, you have two choices. You can retake the test today, during your lunch period, and I'll use that score instead. Or, if you don't feel ready to try again now, I can set you up with a tutoring session, and you can retake the test later in the week and I'll average it in."

I hesitate. I don't want a stupid tutor, but I also don't want to take the test now—lunch will be my best chance to spy on Eva and Amos and see what is going on. And if I bomb the test again, I'm in big trouble. I agree to take the test later in the week. Assuming I do well next time around, my mom will never have to know. Ms. Pinella tells me she will wrangle a tutor to meet with me, and to come back after last bell.

When I step out into the deserted hallway, no one is there. I hesitate, not sure if I should stick around or wait a minute for Cooper. Plastered to the bulletin board is a neon yellow poster for the Environment Club that reads: Rising Seas, a Film About a Growing Menace. Wednesday 4 P.M. BE THERE!

If only a giant tsunami would come along right now and sweep me away so I wouldn't have to retake the math test.

Then I see Cooper, rushing back down the hallway toward me. He waves. "Annalise."

"Where'd you go?" I say, surprised at the peevish tone in my voice.

"Sorry about that. Um, I went to check if Noelle was okay."

"Noelle? Why?" She's not the one who bombed her test. She was the one standing at the board, explaining things to the rest of us.

"She has serious stage fright. Couldn't you tell? I thought she was going to have a coronary up there."

I shrug. "I guess." A twinge of jealousy pinches my heart. I can't believe I care, that he rushed off to check on her, but I do. Have I made a big mistake, blowing off Cooper all this time for a fantasy, something that didn't exist? Now, it was probably too late.

Except he'd come back. There was that. "Pinella is giving me a retake. Hopefully I don't bomb the next one, too. I was a little off Friday."

"Yeah, I heard," he says, making me wonder how much he'd heard. About me getting stood up, too? At least he's not lecturing me for stupidly turning down his offer for a study date. "So, Eva actually won those tickets? Crazy, huh?"

"Yeah. You kind of called that one. Maybe you're psychic." He laughs, but I am confused. Is this why he has hung around waiting for me? To talk about the concert? Or worse, to gloat that I'd been stood up? I think of something to say that will let me retain a shred of dignity. "Actually, you won't believe this—" and I quickly tell him the good news about what happened with Colin Dirge and how he's promised to leave me floor seats.

But instead of looking happy for me, he looks stricken. "Guess you don't need these, then . . ." he says, his words trailing off, and then I look down and see what he's holding out in his hands. A printout for two tickets to the show.

He chuckles softly. "Funny. I, um, scored a couple of comped seats. My cousin's an intern at *Stuff It* magazine and his boss passed them along. I was going to see if maybe . . ."

He holds out the sheet of paper and I inspect the tickets. Funny, they don't look like comped seats, they each have the price $250 printed right on them, and comps typically have no value.

He takes it back, folding the paper and carefully tucking it into his back pocket. "But, I guess you're all set, so maybe I'll just ask someone else."

I'm about to tell him that, although I am touched by his effort, I've already got my plans set. I'm going with . . . well . . . who? I won't be there with Declan, not *my* Declan, who doesn't even really exist anyway, and not with my back-stabbing best friend Maeve, who's probably thrilled that she's off the hook from going to the concert with me, and can now go plot world destruction somewhere with the real Declan.

I think how instead, I could go to the concert with Cooper, who must have heard all the nasty things said about me last year but has never seemed to care. Who has clearly tried so hard to please me, maybe actually spending gobs of money on these seats, but not saying that, so I won't feel obligated to say yes out of guilt. Who will probably take Noelle if I turn him down, which some small evil gremlin living deep down inside me doesn't want to happen.

Plus, at least this time, Cooper's gaze meets me squarely in the eye, not my boobs.

"Wait," I say, spontaneously changing my mind. Why not? "Yes. I'd love to."

"Really?" He smiles in partial disbelief, as the bell rings.

"Really." It's ironic. Only a few days ago, I had no shot at any concert tickets, and now I've got two pairs. We linger, going over travel arrangements, and as he turns to go, I can't help teasing him. "Wait a sec. I thought you hated Brass Knuckles? What happened?" He freezes, and holds my gaze. I expect him to backpedal, to claim he has belatedly discovered Viggo Witts's true genius after watching an episode of Behind the Music.

Instead, he gives me a lopsided grin. "Oh, I still do," he says, leaving me a parting wave and a wink. "With a passion."

CHAPTER 26

NOELLE

I find Amos at his locker after school, fishing through what appears to be a rancid pile of crumpled papers, smelly jockstraps, and chewing tobacco.

"Hey," I say, keeping my distance from the boy-stench. I've waited all day until this moment, knowing this was the best place to corner him, with Eva's locker all the way on the other side of the building.

"Wassup, Noelle." He nods but continues to rummage around, probably thinking I'm just there to deliver a message from Eva. Something simple, like she's running late.

"Amos. I need to talk to you." My voice must reveal some urgency, because now he glances at me expectantly, his forehead crinkling with concern.

Where to begin? I go for a sudden attack, to catch him off guard and force him to reveal the truth. *J'accuse!* I lean in and whisper, "I know what's going on with Annalise."

He flinches a bit at her name, then looks at me blankly. "Annalise Bradley? Um, that's ancient history." He grabs a textbook from a pile and bangs his locker shut, as if to punctuate his words.

"Are you sure?"

He expels a harsh laugh. "Extremely. Eva'd have my balls on a platter if I even glanced twice at that chick." Still, his blue eyes are flecked with concern. Innocent—or not? "Why?" he demands. "What have you heard?"

"It's probably nothing . . ."

"It is nothing. Trust me." His gaze presses into my skull.

"It's just . . ." Now, I squirm uncomfortably. "Something that happened between you two Saturday afternoon? At the Tedeschi's?" Maybe there is some innocent explanation, after all.

Amos shakes his head, relieved. "Not possible. I was away at a soccer match all day. In Duxbury. No lie. You can check the team website. Scored two goals." Something in the way he looks right at me makes me know he is telling me the truth. That his alibi will hold.

"Really?" I blush and now I want to get out of there in the worst way. "My bad, I must have gotten it wrong." I start backing away but he grabs my arm and stops me, indignant.

"Wait, what is she saying?"

"N . . . nothing," I stammer. "She didn't say anything. It's just a dumb misunderstanding."

He sighs heavily, as if bringing up her name releases some toxic fumes. "Look, just between you and me, I do feel bad about what went down with her last year. Her getting trashed afterwards. I didn't mean for that to happen. But I haven't spoken to her since. Seriously."

I nod, knowing what we had done, with our rumors. Well, what he had done. Even if she had tempted him to mess around, he didn't have to go along. It takes two to tango, right?

He gazes at me, as if he can read my mind. Then, he grabs my hand and pulls me closer to him, glancing around the hall to make sure no one is listening. "Noelle, I'm a straight up guy. I wouldn't mess around on someone I'm with, you know?" He speaks low, urgently, as though it's important I understand. It occurs to me that anyone passing could easily misinterpret this discussion as a not-so-innocent rendezvous. It could get back to Eva and then I'd be on the receiving end of her jealous rage. We have to wrap this up, and fast.

But then I tune in to what he is saying. "You know, after Eva told me we were done I was upset. And pretty drunk. But nothing even happened . . ." He trails off, shaking his head in dismay.

"Wait, what do you mean?" I am beyond confused. What does he mean, *we were done*? And what does he mean, *nothing happened*?

"Forget it," he says, stuffing his textbook inside his bag and zipping it back up. "Ask her." I'm not sure who he means. Eva? Or Annalise?

"Amos," I say, but he is already taking off, leaving me standing there, wondering why Eva hadn't told me the whole truth. But more importantly, neither had Annalise. If Amos hadn't gone anywhere near her on Saturday, why did she lie and say that he had?

***

I want to go find Eva and ask what Amos was talking about, but I can't. Ms. Pinella had cornered me in the hallway earlier, delighted that I had signed up in the math department to be a tutor, and asked me to come by after last bell to meet a potential student. So I push my way down the hall toward room #209, against the masses of students trying to head out of the building. Suddenly, I feel a hand in the crowd grabbing me. My heart skips a pump when I realize it is Cooper.

He pulls me to the side of the hall letting everyone stream around us. "I see you've recovered," he smiles. After the debacle in math class, Eva had vanished. But Cooper had barged after me, right into the girls' bathroom, scattering a flock of gossiping seniors like angry wet hens, just so he could tell me that I'd done fine and not to worry about idiots like Tyler Walters.

"Barely," I tell him.

"Good." His eyes dance. Not for me. "She said yes!" he says, waving something in my face.

"Who? What's this?" I am confused for only an instant before my heart sinks, realizing that I am too late, that "she" must be Annalise. "Oh. She did?"

"Yup. We're going to see Brass Knuckles tomorrow night. Thanks to you, No. You were genius. About her doing anything to see the band. My brother got me tickets on StubHub. I had to pawn my Ted Williams baseball card, but whatever, it's worth it, right?"

My mind is trying to process all this. "Wait. She's going to the concert. With you?"

I slump against the wall, and he nods happily.

I feel betrayed. What about Declan? I know he can't go, but how could Annalise just waltz off to the concert with another guy? How could she do this to me—I mean, to him? To us? How dare she cheat on me—on Declan—like that? Was she planning to tell him? Or just never let him know? And why had she lied to him about Amos hitting on her? Suddenly, I am white-hot angry.

"She really said yes? What about that guy? Her online boyfriend?"

Cooper's eyes are dancing with triumph. "I guess she's done with him."

"Wait. Didn't that baseball card come from your dad?" I ask, remembering he'd told me once how much it was probably worth—vintage, from the 1950s, mint condition. How could she let him do that, when she knew how spendy those tickets were, and plus, she already had her own tickets from Colin Dirge?

"Well, yeah," he admits. "But—"

"And you just sold it?"

"Yeah, but I didn't want to put pressure on her, so I told her I got the tickets for free."

"I can't believe you did that!" I say hotly, my voice rising, earning us glances from passersby in the hall, but for once I don't care. "You loved that card."

Cooper seems taken aback by my defense of his former prized possession. "I did. But . . . it's okay."

"It's not okay," I insist. "It's stupid. Selling something you love. To see a band you hate! Why do you have to be so—"

I break off in fury. I can't help but feel betrayed, that he would discard something so dear. Casually trade it in. And for what? A chance at a date with *her*.

"So what?" He tries to grab my arm, to calm me down, but I jerk away. "No!" I choke out, telling him I have to go. I flee down the hall, leaving him standing there, staring after me, forever clueless.

My heart sinks. I've failed. I did everything I could to woo Annalise, and I thought it was working, and yet here she is, still managing to take Cooper away from me.

Eva was right from the start: Annalise Bradley is a girl who can't be trusted. She tried to steal another girl's boyfriend, lied about Amos, backstabbed her own boyfriend. Not to mention won over the only guy I'd ever wanted.

I can't believe I had ever defended her, when what I should have done was defriended her.

CHAPTER 27

ANNALISE

When I get out of my last class, I grab my things and race toward the quad, desperate to try to find one last chance to spy Eva, Tori, and Amos before they leave school. Did my words have any effect? By the time I'd gotten to the cafeteria, they were gone, and I hadn't seen them anywhere together the rest of the day, leaving me with no way of knowing what was up.

At the bottom of the stairwell, I stop short, remembering my stupid promise to Ms. Pinella to come and meet a potential math tutor. I groan, spinning on my heel, and race back up the stairs, my legs burning. When I get to room #209, Ms. Pinella is sitting at her desk, alone, grading papers. She looks up when she spots me standing there, panting.

"Annalise. Good. You're the first one here. Take a seat." She gestures to the chair she has pulled up beside her desk. I slide into it and catch my breath. "I really think this could be a nice match," she says, looking up as someone arrives in the doorway. "Ah, here she is."

I turn and see Noelle Spiers frozen in the doorway.

No way. Nuh-huh. I cross my arms defensively. Min Lee, fine. But I am not getting tutored by that Eva Winters lackey, who's too stuck-up to talk to anyone not in her clique. I eye her suspiciously. Does she know anything about the scam? Probably. For all I know, she could be the brains behind the entire operation.

When my gaze reaches hers, she shoots fumes of pure loathing at me. I can practically taste them from across the room.

Whoa. What did I ever do to *her*?

Ms. P. starts chattering away, oblivious, explaining to Noelle how I could use a review session before my make-up test, and how Noelle would get paid by funding from the math department, and how she hopes we can find a mutual time sometime this week.

But Noelle is abruptly shaking her head and backing away like I am toxic. "I can't," she stammers out. "There's something I've got to do today. Tomorrow, too. Actually, I'm pretty busy all week."

Ms. Pinella looks disappointed. "But you said you were interested—"

Noelle is already inching back toward the door. Her gaze avoids me, and she speaks only to Ms. Pinella. "Sorry. It's all on me. But I just can't."

Something she says plucks a chord of recognition deep inside my head. But what? Before I can figure it out, she turns and flees and Ms. Pinella is sighing and apologizing to me. "I'm sorry, Annalise. This is so unlike Noelle." I shrug and roll my eyes. "Let me talk to a few other students tomorrow. I'm sure we can find you the right match."

"Fine," I say, indifferently, rising to my feet and pulling on my shoulder straps. I don't really want a tutor, anyway. I'm fine studying on my own. When I get out into the hallway, Noelle is long gone. Her reaction was bizarre. That look of hatred. Like I'd just stolen her one true love—

Oh. It slowly dawns on me. That's exactly what I did. It only took me, um, forever, to get it. I did do something to her. Or, took something from her.

Cooper.

I feel a small pang of sympathy, but then push it away. This time, it's definitely not my fault. Cooper's been pursuing me. Cooper isn't her boyfriend. Cooper is free to invite whomever he wants to the concert. I didn't do anything wrong. I've got nothing to feel bad about.

I head outside toward the bus line, where my luck finally turns: I see Amos and Eva standing together by the curb. He seems to pull away, but then Eva is grabbing his hand, hard, smiling up at him, like there is nothing wrong. And then she is shoving her tongue down his throat, and the two of them are sucking face like there's no tomorrow.

I can't believe my eyes.

I watch them squeeze hands, walking toward their buses before they part. I know that somehow, some way, my plan has completely failed. But how? What went wrong? I had been perfectly clear about what happened when I was chatting with Eva last night. Didn't she read a word I wrote?

Or, maybe it's not Eva, a little voice in my head says.

But if "DecOlan" is not Eva, then who? I know one thing for certain: I'm not letting this day end without getting an answer.

CHAPTER 28
NOELLE & ANNALISE

DecOlan: why did you lie to me?
KnuckLise99: why did you lie to *me*?

CHAPTER 29

ANNALISE

KnuckLise99: i know you're not really Declan O'Keefe.
KnuckLise99: or his cousin Eva Winters.
KnuckLise99: SO WHO THE HELL ARE YOU?

All I want now is to know.

For the first time since I found out "DecOlan" was a fake, I feel strong. Ready to fight back. To find out the truth. Last year, I didn't have the courage to stand up to Eva. I just fled. Out of fear. Or shame. But sometimes, when your life hits rock bottom, when there's nothing left to lose, it's possible to be braver than you ever imagined.

KnuckLise99: TELL ME WHO YOU ARE.

Is this someone I know? Don't know? Male? Female? Some crazy Internet stalker? Another frenemy? Who?

Crazy thoughts start swirling through my mind, as everyone in my life comes under suspicion. Could it be Cooper? Romancing me online, playing the devoted fan to counteract all his real life Brass Knuckles insults? Or Amos, secretly still harboring some crush on me after all this time, that he needed to keep secret in the real world? Or even Maeve, concocting this faux romance, as some inane way to revive my faith in the male species? Dredging up a picture of her old camp friend, never thinking I'd actually drag her to Worcester to meet him? And what about the real Declan? Was he in on it from the start?

It could be any of them. It could be all of them. I know I sound insane. But there's only one way to find out.

KnuckLise99: WHO ARE YOU? AND WHY DID YOU DO THIS TO ME?

CHAPTER 30

NOELLE

She knows. She *knows*.

She knows I am not Declan. My whole universe tips off its axis and I grip the sides of my chair for dear life.

How did she finally figure it out? Did someone tip her off? Eva? The real Declan? Or was it me? Did I give it away, make one too many mistakes?

Doesn't matter.

My fury at Annalise fades away, as the truth suddenly becomes clear. All of it.

That story she told me about Amos hitting on her wasn't a lie. It was a test. A test, carefully designed to figure out whether or not it was Eva behind the dirty trick. Amos was telling the truth. He wasn't trying to hit on her. He was innocent.

Annalise wasn't "betraying" Declan when she accepted Cooper's invitation to the concert. She already knew her online boyfriend was a total sham.

That I'm a total sham.

My lungs clench up like I'm in front of the classroom again, only a hundred times worse. It's all on me. I am the one who is scheming and deceptive, not her. I don't deserve her friendship. I don't deserve Cooper. I don't deserve anyone.

Hot tears run down my face and I start typing in a stream of consciousness.

DecOlan: i'm sorry.
DecOlan: i'm so so sorry.

KnuckLise99: WHO ARE YOU???

DecOlan: i never meant
DecOlan: i didn't think
DecOlan: i didn't know

KnuckLise99: WHO ARE YOU??? THAT'S ALL I NEED TO KNOW.

DecOlan: just let me explain.

KnuckLise99: WHO ARE YOU??? WHO ARE YOU??? WHO ARE YOU???

I am trembling in fear, even though she has no way to see me, touch me, shake me. I can't tell her who I really am. The minute I tell her, she'll be out of here. Gone. That's the only leverage I have to keep her talking. To make her understand.

DecOlan: i'm someone who wishes i could take it all back.

No reply. Then.

KnuckLise99: why?

Why did we do it? I have no good explanation. The reason no longer seems to exist, if it ever did.

DecOlan: it was over something stupid. it doesn't matter.

Pause.

KnuckLise99: no.
KnuckLise99: why do you wish you could take it all back?

DecOlan: you know why.

Another pause.

KnuckLise99: i don't know anything.
KnuckLise99: i thought i did.
KnuckLise99: i trusted you.
KnuckLise99: i told you things.
KnuckLise99: everything.

DecOlan: i know.

KnuckLise99: it was all a joke to you.

DecOlan: it was never that.
DecOlan: it was unspeakable.
DecOlan: unforgivable.
DecOlan: indefensible.
DecOlan: but never a joke.

KnuckLise99: do i know you? do you know me? who are you?

DecOlan: who i am was a lie
DecOlan: but what i said was true.
DecOlan: what we had
DecOlan: that much was real.

KnuckLise99: no. you lied.
KnuckLise99: all along.
KnuckLise99: why should I believe you?
KnuckLise99: you won't even tell me who you are. you owe me that much.

DecOlan: i'll tell you.
DecOlan: i will.
DecOlan: just promise.
DecOlan: after i do.
DecOlan: you'll listen.
DecOlan: not leave.

I see that she is typing something, then erasing it. Then typing, then erasing. My heart dangles in midair. Then it falls when I read her reply.

KnuckLise99: don't bother.
KnuckLise99: i won't believe you.
KnuckLise99: you could say you're anyone.
KnuckLise99: play me some more.
KnuckLise99: more lies.
KnuckLise99: I'm done.

She's right. Why should she trust me?

DecOlan: wait. please.
DecOlan: you're right.

DecOlan: i'm sorry.
DecOlan: you have every right to hate me.
DecOlan: just let me come to you.
DecOlan: explain in person.
DecOlan: face-to-face.

KnuckLise99: NO WAY.
KnuckLise99: r u kidding?
KnuckLise99: to my house?
KnuckLise99: you could be anyone.
KnuckLise99: a psycho.
KnuckLise99: some lunatic.

DecOlan: somewhere public?
DecOlan: somewhere safe.
DecOlan: tomorrow.
DecOlan: at the concert.
DecOlan: meet me at Will Call.

KnuckLise99: no way.
KnuckLise99: why should i?
KnuckLise99: why would i?

DecOlan: let me make it right.
DecOlan: please.
DecOlan: give me that chance.
DecOlan: let me show you what we had meant something
DecOlan: i don't deserve that much but you do.
DecOlan: i promise i'll make it up to you.

I wait for her reply. I know it's a long shot, but if I can just convince her to meet me, maybe I can make this right. Maybe, just maybe, I won't have to lose her. Because if I finally know my one true desire, I also know Annalise's: to meet Viggo Witts.

And I can give that to her. But only if she'll agree to come.

I stare at the screen, willing her to answer yes.

I wait and wait and wait and wait. An eternity tumbles by. Then finally, I see she is writing her response.

KnuckLise99: i'll see you there.

My heart collapses in relief. She will. She will meet me. I reach out to thank her, to promise her this time, I will keep my word. Then all of a sudden, up pops an error message I've never seen before. Something's not right. I don't need someone from the Genius Bar to tell me something is very, very wrong. I hit refresh and this time, am bounced back to the homepage.

"No!" I pound the keyboard in frustration.

I attempt to log in as Declan half a dozen times, frantically, pushing shift, caps lock, number lock, and anything else I can think to try to get back to Annalise, to confirm that I will see her there. But each time, I only get this response:

User Name Unknown.
Password Incorrect.
Please Try Again.

CHAPTER 31

ANNALISE

Meet him? Is he insane? And he thinks he can make this up to me? Part of me wants to tell this so-called "DecOlan" that there's no way I'm meeting him anywhere, ever. But halfway through our conversation, the truth hit me: I'll never believe what I read on my screen. What if this is my only chance to find out who he actually is? The only way to know for sure is face-to-face. My fingers race across the keyboard.

KnuckLise99: i'll see you there.

Silently, I finish the sentence to myself: *But you won't see me.*

But before he can reply, our entire conversation suddenly disappears. I scroll up but it is gone. All of it. I click over to Declan's profile, but he is gone, too.

Vanished. Into cyberspace.

Weird. I sit there for a minute, refreshing the screen, trying to figure out what could have happened. Slowly, it dawns on me that maybe that's my answer. Whoever "DecOlan" was has freaked out, bailed, gone rogue. That apology, that promise to make it up to me, all just a sham. Buying time to go delete the account. Why hadn't I just kept demanding his name? Threatened to turn him in? Maybe he—or was it a she?—would have finally confessed. Now it was too late.

The adrenaline from our online shouting match slowly drains from my system. Probably it was just some crazy troll. Some creepy forty-year-old pedophile, trying to lure me in. Maybe I'd dodged a bullet. Good thing I'd refused to have him come over here, to an empty house.

Then, all of sudden, my phone rings. I look at it, startled. My caller ID reads: O'Keefe. Impossible. Freaky.

"Hello?" I say warily. My throat is tight again. Breathless.

A boy's voice on the line. Familiar.

"Annalise?"

"Yeah?"

"This is Declan. Declan O'Keefe?"

His voice is high, nervous, as if he's never called a girl on the phone before. "Maeve's friend. From Worcester?"

Oh. Him.

"Hey." My hopes come crashing down. Why is he calling me? After all, isn't he supposed to be all into Maeve?

"I'm sorry, but I thought you should know—I contacted tech support and reported that account fraudulent."

What the what?

"You did what?" I nearly shout.

"Yeah, sorry," he says. "Look, I know you didn't want me to tell my parents or Eva, and I didn't, but I really hated the idea of someone impersonating me online. Freaks me out. I mean, identity fraud is a serious issue and I just wanted you to know, in case you were still getting messages from that impostor, that it's over. I just got an e-mail from tech support. They've deleted the account."

I don't know whether to be irritated or relieved. So it was the real Declan, not the fake one, that just cut the cord. That means whoever it was is forever lost to me now. No way to find out who they were, what they wanted to tell me, why they did what they did. Unless they really do show up at Will Call.

I try to focus on what Declan is telling me: that online identity fraud is actually a misdemeanor in our state, and the site administrators would investigate who was behind it and he could even press charges, but since it's his cousin, he'd rather not, if that was all right with me.

"Actually," I interrupt him, "I don't think it's Eva."

He sounds startled. "It's not? Then who?"

That's what I'd like to know. "I don't know. Wait." I realize this might be a chance to find out the difference between the real Declan and "DecOlan." I doubt anyone could just make up all that stuff on the spot—some of it was probably taken from the person's own life story. Was any of it real?

"Can I ask you some questions?"

"Sure," he says cautiously.

"So, you're Declan O'Keefe, and you really won the Worcester County Chess Tournament when you were eleven, right?"

"Um, yeah. How'd you—"

"And your dad Patrick is a software engineer."

"Correct."

I mentally scroll through all the other stories "DecOlan" had shared with me.

"And you used to sing chorus and one time you got so nervous during a solo that you choked?"

"Um, what?"

"You used to do chorus?"

"Uh, no."

Bingo! Gotcha! So that might be something real. What else?

"And did you ever push your mom and accidentally break her wrist?"

"What? No! Of course not," he says indignantly. "Why?"

"I'm just trying to sort out the truth," I tell him and explain what I'm doing.

"Look, what that person did was crazy town. Who knows if anything they told you was fiction or fantasy? It'll probably never make sense. I think you should just forget it. So does Maeve."

Maeve. So clearly, they've been in touch.

"What did she say?" Had she told him we'd fought? Over him?

"Nothing. I don't know. You should talk to her," he stammers. "She said you're still going to that concert together, right?"

"I'm not sure." I realize I haven't even told Maeve about Cooper's invitation and my acceptance. "I actually may be going with someone else."

"Well, that's too bad, she's a great girl. She used to talk about you all the time, at camp, you know. My best friend, Annalise. The future Olympic gymnast."

"She did?"

"Yeah. She said you used to put on shows for all the neighborhood kids."

It was true. I'd perform flips and back handsprings in our backyard for anyone Maeve could round up, acting as my coach, sports agent, and publicist all rolled into one. But that was pre-boobs, pre-boys, back when life was a whole lot less complicated. Sometimes, I wish the carousel of time would just stop and let me off.

"I can't believe you remember that," I say, a little embarrassed.

"Well, I guess I remember everything Maeve said." He pauses, and coughs, and I can figure out the rest for myself: how he has been crushing on Maeve since forever but was all elbows and knees. "She never really noticed me," he says quietly. "She was obsessed with Aiden Sylvester."

That was true. Every summer, it seemed, Maeve came home having gone one base further with Aiden.

"Not anymore," I inform him. "He hooked up with Faye Snowe the last night of camp."

"Really?"

"Um, yeah." Wow was this guy clueless. How could anyone go to Camp Chicawawa and not know this? Maeve and I had only dissected the cheating episode nightly for all of Labor Day weekend.

But his words remind me what a true friend Maeve has always been. Why had I stopped valuing her and turned to some online surrogate friendship? Because she was busy with volleyball? Because she had a life? She was still always there for me. Going to a concert she had no interest in seeing. Traveling to smelly old Worcester. Helping me concoct my crazy revenge scheme. And what had I done? Been judgy about her little sister's dumb decision. Jealous that she was interested in a boy I had no legitimate claim on. Which, in a way, made me no different than Eva Winters. It's like I was so scared of losing her, instead, I starting pushing her away first. Lately, I've been completely in my own head. Having an identity crisis. Obsessing over the band and their music and . . . hello!

Something in my brain clicks. Why didn't I think of it before? There is a way to help Samantha. And to make it up to Maeve.

"Listen, Declan, I gotta go," I say breathlessly, my mind tallying up what I will need. Some red lipstick. A mirror. My digital camera. Will it work? Will it be enough to make her forgive me? Maybe. But there's one thing more I can do. "But it's fine with me if you want to ask Maeve out."

"Sweet!" He cackles a weird laugh, and my resentment towards Maeve instantly dissolves. No, I definitely don't want to keep Declan to myself. Besides, Cooper Franklin just might turn out to be more than meets the eye.

"No, you two are made for each other," I say firmly. "Plus, I've got the perfect first date in mind."

CHAPTER 32

NOELLE

I've called a Code Red, texting for Eva and Tori to meet me in the girls' bathroom before first period so I can tell them in person what happened. This emergency can only be conveyed in real life. From here on out, we're going off the grid. I'm paranoid that any more online communication could be tracked and used against us.

"You guys. She knows."

"What? Who?" Tori asks, unable to resist stealing a glance at herself in the grimy mirror. "Who knows what?"

But Eva understands exactly what I am talking about.

"How?"

"I don't know. But she's definitely figured out Declan's a fake." I tell them how Annalise had seemingly discovered the truth and demanded I tell her who I am, but then the account froze and disappeared.

"Well don't look at me. I didn't do it," Eva says, implying I thought that she was the one this time who somehow locked me out of the account. "You said you could handle it without us, remember?"

Tori looks panicked. "Does she know it's us?"

"Not yet."

"Thank god." Eva sighs in relief and Tori's frown fades.

"But I'm going to tell her the truth."

They both stare at me and Eva finally asks, "Are you high? Seriously, Noelle. Why would you do that if she has no idea it's us?"

"Tell me what really happened, the night Amos and Annalise hooked up," I say, brusquely changing the subject.

"What?" My question catches Eva off guard. "What does that have to do with anything?"

"It does, just answer the question."

"Why?" she grimaces. "Was she talking about that? Did she tell you something different? I knew you were—"

"No. He did."

She frowns, quickly figuring out who I mean. "You spoke to Amos? Behind my back?"

"I had to. It was obvious you hadn't told me the whole story. He said to talk to you. Did you tell him the two of you were done?"

I've thought and thought about what Amos said, what he was hinting at, and only one thing makes sense. But I need to hear it from her.

And she starts to explain. "I don't know what I told him. I was, like, mad at him, over something stupid, I don't even remember, and I walked out of the dance. Next thing I know, I'm getting texts that he's in the stairwell, hooking up with someone else. That skank."

"Wait. Back up. So, you, like, broke up with him that night?" Tori asks. I stare at Eva, waiting to hear her reply.

I flash back to Annalise's words that never made sense to me, until now: *i'd see that asshole crying and keep on walking.* And Amos's words: *nothing even happened.* If that was all true, if Eva had dumped him, if he was crying, if Annalise was just trying to comfort him? If maybe she had never even hooked up with him at all, then really, she had done nothing wrong. All of Eva's anger toward her was understandable, sure, but somewhat unjust. Maybe I could even convince Eva to let it go already. To understand why we owed Annalise an apology.

But she is not giving up that easily. "I might have told him we were done," Eva says testily. "So? That doesn't mean it was okay for her to come up and make a move on him. Like, the body wasn't even cold yet. Right guys? I don't get what this has to do with anything."

Tori is nodding slowly, like she sees Eva's point, but I don't agree.

"Because it changes things, Eva," I say, summoning up my courage. "It's not the same, if she thought you guys had broken up, if that's what Amos was telling her."

But Eva digs in her heels. "I don't care what she says. He was still with me. We were just fighting, like couples do. She should have known that. She took advantage of him, all drunk and upset. And she's been playing the victim ever since, like he took advantage of her virtue. Puh-leeze."

"So you let everyone believe the worst? Even though Amos says nothing even happened. That they were just talking."

Her face flushes with anger. "My ass they were just talking. I don't care what he says. Amanda said they were practically all over each other. Or would have been, if they weren't interrupted. Besides, what was I going to do? Let the whole school find out I dumped him, but he's hooking up one second later with someone else. Humiliate me like that? No way."

I can't believe I had ever swallowed that this was at all for my benefit, to help me with Cooper. This whole stupid vendetta was always about one thing: her pride.

"Well, it's not right. And now, it's over. You want to know why I'm telling her? That's why."

"So what, you're choosing her—over us?" Her eyes are suddenly hurt, wounded.

"It's not like that," I say quietly, although I know it is. "I have to make it right." I just hope my dad will agree to drive me to the concert tonight once I tell him the whole story.

"No way. It's not just up to you. This could get us so busted. All of us. Right, Tori?"

We both turn to see what Tori thinks. But she is no longer listening to either of us. Tori is staring down at her phone's screen, with a puzzled expression on her face, rapidly scrolling down with her thumb.

Then, her beautiful face twists in anger and she shouts, "Holy crap!"

CHAPTER 33

ANNALISE

Maeve is waiting for me at school Tuesday morning when I get off my bus. "Lise, how'd you do it?" Her voice rings with glee. To my relief, any hard feelings between us seem to be forgotten. "The feed has totally been hacked."

"Who says it was me?" I say, giving her a faux innocent expression.

"Please," she grins. "Who else?"

I had realized there was one group I could tap that would rally behind Samantha's cause. The Brass Knuckles fans. Duh. I had grabbed a tube of red lipstick and carefully written the chorus from "Inner Beauty" on my bathroom mirror. Then, I had snapped a picture and uploaded the image onto the fan feed, writing: Someone called an eleven-year-old girl UGLY in this online beauty pageant. But I think the pageant organizers are the truly ugly ones. Don't you?

People I had never even met—led by Juniper77 and DaisyFlour84—had all rallied behind the cause, tweeting and retweeting my message on a whole bunch of platforms. When I last checked before going to sleep, there had been about a hundred favorites, which I thought was pretty good. Enough to serve as an apology to Maeve, at least.

"Have you checked it today?"

"No. Why?" I'd completely forgotten I had a quiz first period in Spanish, so I'd spent the entire ride to school frantically conjugating verbs.

"Look!" She holds out her phone. "Look at it now!" I can see to my disbelief that Tori's *InstaHotOrNot* feed has received 42,989 uploads of the Brass Knuckles' song lyrics I'd scrawled on the mirror last night:

A pretty face
does not mean
a pretty heart

Plus, my message has spawned a whole slew of similar mantras. People around the planet have been chiming in with words of their own:

Beautiful people are not always good,
but good people are always beautiful

A beautiful exterior does not mean a beautiful interior

Pretty is as pretty does

Beauty is only skin deep.

"And did you see this?" Maeve adds, showing me dozens of spinoff hashtags have been created, like #StopTorisPageant and #TorisPageantSucks. To be honest, it looks like the whole thing has spun a little out of control. People have uploaded photos of pigs with tiaras, and a trio of boys mooning the camera, and even one of Tori obviously lifted from an old middle school yearbook, looking dorky with bangs and braces.

"Oh my god," I say with a nervous laugh, thankful Tori and I don't share a class. I wouldn't want to get in her path today. "She must be out for blood."

Maeve chortles as she wipes off her glasses. "She can't delete it all fast enough. It just keeps coming and coming."

It turns out, Tori D'Fillipo may have a lot of online friends, but few true fans.

"So, thanks. From me. And Samantha."

"I'm sorry for what I said."

Maeve shrugs, accepting the apology. "But we still need to out who's been playing you. If it wasn't Eva . . ."

Now that we're talking again, I'm bursting to tell her the news about what happened. "It's over. I confronted DecOlan last night, said I knew the whole thing was a fake."

"Did you find out who it was?" Maeve asks, shocked.

"Not exactly," I admit and explain the rest: how the person apologized and asked me to meet up at the concert before we got cut off. Then I tell her my plan. "It's the only way to find out for sure. Since apparently, *your* Declan got the account deactivated."

She nods, like the news doesn't surprise her. "He said he might. But, he's not my Declan."

"He's more yours than mine," I concede.

"We'll see," she says with a mischievous smile. "But from now on—sisters before misters?"

"Always."

"And I hear you're buying my forgiveness with a pair of tickets?" I had told Declan last night that he and Maeve should use the spare set and come to the concert with me and Cooper.

"Exactly."

"I can't believe you're ditching me to go with Cooper Franklin, though. After all that? Perhaps the lady doth protest too much?"

"Perhaps," I admit. "He still says he hates Viggo Witts, you know."

"Yes, but he lurves you." She makes kissy faces at me and I have to threaten to punch her to get her to stop.

"So, are you psyched for the show?" Maeve asks.

"Totally," I lie. To be honest, the thrill has been overshadowed by everything else. The prospect of coming face-to-face with my online enemy. The disappointment over Declan. Eva snagging the chance to sing on stage. But still, I remind myself, there will be Viggo, his amazing silken voice, the band, the music . . .

"What about you? Have I turned you into a Viggo fan?" I tease her.

She scrunches up her face in horror. "Nah, he's still kind of a tool. But, well, his fans are okay." She starts telling me how a bunch of them are planning to meet up at intermission to hold an "Inner Beauty" sing-a-thon to raise money for the Changing Faces charity.

It's amusing, seeing Maeve lose her famous cool and get all enthusiastic over something, at last. She'd deny it with her dying breath, but it's true: wry, sarcastic Maeve Rosen has turned into the biggest Knucklie I know.

CHAPTER 34

NOELLE

Eva escorts Tori down to the nurse's office so she can lie down until her mom can come pick her up. For the rest of the day, the whole school is buzzing with rumors: a) that Anonymous is behind her site getting hacked; b) that one of the pageant losers attempted suicide; c) that Tori has attempted suicide; d) that Viggo Witts is suing Tori for copyright infringement; e) that the whole thing is a stunt for a new reality TV show.

None of which is true. The principal establishes that all of it had taken place off school grounds and washes his hands of the matter by noon. Most people remain clueless as to who got the viral campaign started, but it's pretty obvious to me. I mean, you only have to look at the words on the screen to figure it out.

After school, Eva is waiting for me at the bike racks outside the building. "Poor Tori," she says, shaking her head in disbelief. "It's so messed up."

"I guess," I shrug, glad this happened before my mom's company got involved. Honestly, I can't muster up much sympathy for the pageant's demise; it always seemed that it churned out more grief than good.

Just then, we spot Maeve and Annalise leaving the building and skipping towards the buses. They look triumphant, giggling and excited. Happy to be together. Friends. They're all Eva and I are not.

Eva stiffens. "Look at them. We are so getting them back."

But I am done fighting Eva's fight. Where will it end? World World Three? Armageddon? "No," I shake my head. "I'm out."

"Really? So what, you're going to let her get away with this? Humiliating our friend? Taking your man? Seriously, Noey, you're a lost cause. I'm tired of sticking up for you. I've been doing it forever and I'm sick of it. You let people walk all over you. When are you ever going to stand up for yourself?"

Her question rings in my ears, a challenge. But for some reason, the thought of losing her doesn't scare me. Not anymore. Maybe because I already have, in a way. Like my mom, I want to be able to stand on my own two feet. Like my dad, I want to find the courage to say I quit. I put the two together and summon up the words I've been wanting to say to her for a long time.

"Now. I'm standing up for myself right now."

From here on out, I am going to tell Eva what I really think. Right to her face. Even if it kills me. Or our friendship.

Then I tell her exactly what she's going to do and why she's going to do it. That if she does the one thing I ask, I'll take the blame for what we did. But if not, I'll make sure Annalise turns all three of us in.

"After that? You and me? We're done. I quit."

She looks confused for a second, then a flash of recognition of what my words mean.

"You can't do that," she sputters as I hop on my bike. "You can't go and quit a friendship."

"Oh yeah? Watch me."

***

I enjoy the memory of Eva's stunned face the whole ride home. When I get there, my parents are both waiting for me at the front door. At first, I am happy to see them. I can't wait to tell my dad what happened today. I know he'll be proud I've finally stood up to Eva and ended our friendship.

Then I see that my mom has her arms crossed, and my dad has an uncharacteristic frown on his gentle face.

"What?" I nervously wheel my bike closer to the house. What could be so dire that they're both standing outside waiting for me? Then I know. I feel it in my gut. This is it. The Big D talk. They've decided to tell me today. About the divorce.

"Noelle," my dad says. "We need to speak to you. Now."

"Don't," I say, shakily, not ready to launch into this right now. Every person on the planet knows how this conversation starts: *You know your mother and I love you very much . . .* "You can't just split up because things are a little tough."

My parents blink at each other, confused.

My dad shakes his head. "Who's splitting up?"

"You two?" I ask uncertainly.

"Not that I'm aware of," my mom says, looking aghast, as my dad shakes his head for her benefit, only stronger this time.

"Then what?"

"We need to know who the hell is Declan O'Keefe? And why have you been impersonating him online?"

***

After I break down in tears, after I tell my parents why I thought they were getting a divorce, and after my dad assures me they are not, after he explains going solo just meant he had been talking to an old lawyer buddy named Bob Pontin about incorporating his accounting business as a solo practitioner, and my mom assures me she had no agenda beyond old-school feminism, I admit the truth about what I had been doing to Annalise.

They get very quiet and finally explain how they found out. My dad got a call from the website's tech support about a report of a fraudulent account that was traced primarily to our IP address. They were able to send my dad everything, every single conversation that took place between us. They told him that this could potentially involve charges or a civil suit. And now, the way he is lecturing me, I have a feeling I might never be allowed out of the house again, let alone let out tonight for the concert. My parents pepper me with guilt-laden accusations that set my pulse pounding.

"Do you realize how serious this is?"

"That the police could arrest you for impersonation?"

"That this could ruin your future?"

They don't bring up faith, morality, or how I've disappointed Pastor Reilly and the entire heavenly bodies, but I can't help but feel as though I have. I bow my head, too ashamed to look them in the eye.

"Luckily for you, the boy whose identity you stole has opted not to press charges," my dad says dryly. "For now."

So Declan O'Keefe, the real one, Eva's cousin, has figured it out as well.

"So tell me again, from the beginning, exactly why you girls thought of this bright idea to masquerade as a boy and devastate this poor girl?"

I don't know what to say, it all sounds small minded when I replay it to myself. Because Annalise once almost hooked up with Eva's boyfriend while they were having a fight, or were broken up, depending on who you believed? Because I thought distracting Annalise would give me a shot with Cooper? And furthermore, what sounds really idiotic: that I ended up befriending her, even though the whole time I was also betraying her?

"I don't know," I whisper.

"You don't know?"

So I tell them the whole story. How I had gone along with it and how I regretted it right from the start. How I had finally stood up to Eva. How Annalise had found out the truth. And how I wanted, no, needed, to make it right, but tonight was my only chance. I tell them everything, knowing with every word I say I'm more likely to get grounded exactly like "DecOlan,"—oh, the irony!—my phone, my freedom, stripped away.

And then I tell them what I've sworn to do, knowing in my heart there is no way they'll ever let me see it through.

CHAPTER 35

ANNALISE

"Annalise? You almost ready?"

My mom calls up to me as I'm finishing getting dressed for the concert.

Despite what I told Maeve earlier, I am actually starting to get pretty excited. Cooper and Maeve will be here any minute. My mom insisted on driving the three of us down to the arena—all along, she has been dubious that these tickets really existed, unclear why some old roadie would just give me tickets like that, convinced there must be some catch. She's still suspicious, even after I'd shown her my text message exchange with Colin, nervously reminding him about the promised tickets, and his curt reply: yup.

When I finally come down to the living room, she looks nice. Too nice. For her job, my mom normally wears her short hair pulled back, no makeup, and sensible white sneakers. Tonight, she is wearing a red silk dress, and her hair is fluffed up and she has even put on shimmery eye makeup, which gives her the look of a raccoon.

"Why are you so dressed up?" I ask, and she actually blushes.

"I'm going out for dinner."

"Tonight?"

"In the city. While you're at the concert. What, did you think I was going to just sit in the parking lot by myself all night long until you were done?"

Honestly, that's exactly what I'd figured my mother would do, but I guess that's not the most thrilling use of her time. "No, but—"

"Oh! Before I forget." She picks up a small FedEx box sitting by the stack of mail on the foyer table. "This came. For you."

I look at the return address. North Carolina. Dad. "What is it?"

She smiles mysteriously. "I don't know. Why don't you open it and see?"

I pick curiously at the packing tape, trying to get it open. So Dad did get me something, too, not just Elena. "So, who exactly are you going to dinner with? Diane?"

"No," she says a little too casually. "With Gerald."

"Gerald?" I say dubiously, trying out the name. A very masculine sounding name. Is my mother going on a date?

She continues, ignoring me. "Actually, it's a funny story. Remember when I crashed the car? Well, Gerald's the regional manager for Enterprise. He helped me get my rental all straightened out with the insurance company. And then he asked me out. We've gone on two dinner dates so far. And one brunch. He's really nice. A modest, unassuming guy."

I am shocked. What did they do with my mother, the queen of bitter? "Dates?" I repeat. "But you never go on dates."

"I know," she says. And then she giggles in this lame girlish voice.

So this is why my mom's brain has been in la la land lately. I make a mental note to text Elena later and tell her that our mother doesn't have a thyroid disorder or an ovarian cyst; she has a *boyfriend*.

"Why didn't you tell me?" I manage to say.

My mother takes in my betrayed expression. "I didn't know what you might say."

"Me?"

"Look, I know you've heard me being down on men, after your father, holding what your dad did against everyone else. But I can't stay that way forever. Pushing people away. It's not healthy."

"I guess."

She looks at me critically. "And I don't want that attitude rubbing off on you."

"What do you mean?" I say, although I know exactly what she means. I never told my mother anything about what happened with Amos, but somehow deep down I wonder if she somehow has a clue.

"You should be having fun. Enjoying opportunities."

"I am!"

"Then tell me about this Cooper." I guess she figures she's shown me hers, now I'll show her mine. "You've never mentioned him before."

But I'm not laying down all my cards just yet. "He's okay, I guess. Plays lacrosse. Smart in math. Goes to church. A parent's dream."

She frowns, as if she's disappointed he doesn't ride a Harley and have multiple tats. "Wow. That's a real ringing endorsement."

"Sorry, next time I'll be sure to bring home a meth-head," I say wryly.

She sighs. "Not funny."

I finally peel away enough tape so I can pry the box open. The present is wrapped up in tissue paper, and sitting on top is a note. "Honey, saw this and thought of you. Enjoy the concert tonight! Love, Dad."

Wow again. I glance at my mom, suddenly feeling wretched that I had blown him off, and touched that he would still make the effort. I feel so undeserving, I don't even want to unwrap it. "I never called him back," I admit, passing the note to her, letting the box sit there on my lap.

"I know, I told him you were all wrapped up in this concert stuff and your math test this week," my mom says gently, still in the dark about all the Declan drama I'd been going through as well. "But see!" She exhales a big sigh, gesturing to the mystery package. "He's trying, isn't he?"

"Yeah. He is."

"Well, let's see what he got you then."

Excited, I finally reach inside, push aside the layers of paper, and pull out a crisp white T-shirt, tightly rolled up and tied with a piece of twine. Could it be? I could even wear it tonight!! "Mom, look!" I pick open the knot, and the T-shirt rolls open. But instead of Viggo Witts, the face of Ramon, the lead guitarist of the Be Bop Brothers, is staring back at me.

WTF?

My mom and I stare at it silently for a long moment. Her face twists with anguish, like here comes another time that she has to apologize to me for *your father's* many failings. That she ever married him. That he cheated. That he left us.

But instead of feeling anger or disappointment, something else bubbles up inside me. Laughter. My dad's attempt is just so lame. Like no matter how hard he tries, he's doomed to botch things. My sister's unintended words float back to me: *Maybe he'll surprise you.* The absurdity of the situation takes hold of me, and before I know it, I start to snicker, and pretty soon I'm rolling on the floor in full-on gut-busting laughter. I can't keep blaming my dad for his weaknesses. Expecting him to be more than he is. Elena is right. I have to let it go.

"What's so funny?" my mom demands, looking somewhat relieved at my bizarre reaction.

"Dad . . . he's just so clueless," I manage to gasp out. "What you were saying. Nobody's perfect, right?" Maybe my dad won't ever get it right, but at least he's trying. And if my mom can give this Gerald a chance, maybe I can again, too. If not with Declan, then maybe with Cooper.

She smiles in confused relief as the doorbell rings. She reaches it first, since I'm still on the floor trying to compose myself, and pulls the door open. Cooper is standing on the doorstep with an adorably nervous smile, with Maeve beside him. Both are grinning at me. My eyes travel downward, and I see they have each pinned buttons to their shirts with the face of Viggo Witts and his slogan "Keeping it real."

"I got them on eBay," Maeve explains, pinning one to my sweater.

"I'm almost ready, can you guys just give me five more minutes?" I call out to them, grabbing my phone and dashing upstairs. I have a one call to make before we go.

The least I can do is tell my dad thanks for the shirt.

CHAPTER 36

NOELLE

"Thirty minutes," my dad says sternly. He pulls into the parking lot of the arena. Crowds of girls my age stream around us, most wearing Knucklies T-shirts and jeans, heading inside. "Understand? Find her, make your apology, tell her you are grounded for what you did, and then come back here and we'll go right home."

"I get it," I say, shaking my head in agreement. I'm just thankful my parents agreed to let me come tonight at all. My mom didn't want to let me do this, but Dad had talked her into it, saying it was the right thing to do, that this girl was going to be standing there waiting for me and I had a moral obligation to fulfill.

"I'll be waiting. Right here."

I hesitate. What if Annalise refuses me? What if it takes longer to convince her? "But what if—"

"Just text me if there's a problem." He pulls out his book, *The Dummies' Guide to Starting a Business*, curtly ending the conversation.

I sigh. I may be in the doghouse, but at least my parents can't go and divorce me. I head toward the main lobby, where I told Eva to meet me. I spot her easily through the crowd. Eva is way overdressed for a concert, stuffed into a slinky black dress and teetering on wedge heels, hanging on to Amos for support. I see what I have come for: the laminated VIP passes, hanging from thick lanyards around their necks. On the passes are shimmering hologram images of Viggo Witts's face. They stop in front of me. I gaze evenly at Eva. Is she ready to hand hers over?

Amos doesn't seem clued into the tension between us. "Hey, Noelle! How'd you get tickets?"

"Someone had an extra," I gesture vaguely to the Will Call window. "But first, Eva—"

"Noey, can I talk to you for a second? In private?" Eva's voice is cheerful, but only on the surface. "Amos, we'll be right back."

"What, now?" Amos asks, incredulous.

"It's female stuff." She digs her fingernails into my arm and drags me outside towards the steps. As soon as we are out of his sight, she pulls me to a stop. "I can't believe you're really going through with this," she hisses. "I've been thinking about this all day. You said the account is deactivated. History. She'll never figure out it was us. So what's the point of telling her now?"

"It's too late," I say. "Your cousin knows his identity was hacked. And now my parents know. Declan called it in and the site traced all our chats to me. It's all going to come out eventually. But the point is, she has a right to know."

For once, she is speechless, probably shocked that I am not backing down. I put out my hand and she reluctantly pulls the VIP pass from her neck and gives it to me. I had told her if she let me have it, I would take all the blame for what we'd done and leave her and Tori out of it. But if she didn't, I'd encourage Annalise to turn all three of us in.

"Fine." Her tone turns disdainful. "You really think this will make her forgive you? That she won't turn on you, too? Look what she and her friend just did to Tori. She's really got you brainwashed. Just like Tori said."

No, I think. You are the one who has been brainwashed, by a shiny new friend who has twisted your spunk into spite.

"She won't," I tell her.

"How do you know for sure?"

I don't. But it's a risk I have to take. "I'm telling her the truth. And don't worry. I'll say it was all on me."

"Telling who the truth?" a voice behind us asks. Amos. We both turn slowly. He must have wandered outside and come upon our heated discussion without us noticing. "Telling who the truth?" he repeats.

"No one," Eva says quickly.

But I am done with staying silent. "No, tell him," I say. "Or I will. It's all because of him, anyway. He has a right to know."

Eva's face twists defensively. "It was just a dumb prank."

"What was?" Amos asks slowly, and when I tell him the whole story, how Eva had used her cousin Declan's profile to catfish Annalise, publicly humiliate her at the mall, and then spread rumors that her online boyfriend was just a fantasy, I don't think I've ever seen him so angry. He peppers us with questions that I try to answer, while Eva just stands there, dumbly, as the crowd streams around the three of us.

Finally, he turns to Eva, eyeing her as if for the first time. "Who *are* you?"

She looks stunned, reaching for him. "Amos—"

"No, I don't even want to know." He snaps her hands off his wrist like he's flinging a Frisbee. "I can't believe you're still messing with that poor girl. It was bad enough all the rumors that got started, after I told you nothing happened. Plus, you dumped me that night! Maybe we should have left it that way."

"Amos. Wait."

He rips the VIP lanyard off his neck, then fumbles around and grabs something from his pocket. His ticket. "Enjoy the show," he says, thrusting them both at Eva. "I'm through with you. For good."

He spins and charges into the crowd like a mad bull stampeding through the streets of Pamplona. Eva gives me a look of anguish before she yells, "Amos," and starts chasing after him.

CHAPTER 37

ANNALISE

"There he is!"

I turn and see Declan waving madly at Maeve and me, right where we'd told him to meet us, outside the arena in front of the Golden Greek statue.

"Hey," Maeve says shyly, and I am amused to see how excited she looks to see him. "Sorry we're late." We introduce the guys, who shake hands heartily, although Cooper's grip leaves Declan tenderly wringing out his fingers afterwards when he thinks no one is looking.

"Where to?" Declan asks, looking around like Bambi who'd wandered into a den of iniquity.

"First concert, Dec?" Maeve teases him.

"Of course not!" he says, full of mock indignation. "My parents took me to the Beach Boys reunion tour last summer."

I expect her to make a snarky comment, but instead Maeve surprises me. "The Beach Boys rule!" she squeals, then shoots me a look that says, don't you even.

"Maeve and I can go to Will Call to pick up the tickets," I suggest, pointing to the long sea of bodies snaking out the door. "How about you guys go grab us two T-shirts and we'll meet you over there?"

The guys amiably agree, and shuffle off toward the merchandise booths, while Maeve and I find our way to the end of the line.

"So. Any good vibrations yet?" I ask, teasing her about her and Declan's lack of musical taste. "Still planning to kidnap the Kardashian kid?"

"Nah, we've moved on to the royal princess," she says, ever unflappable. "So how about you and Cooper? Are you actually going to give him a chance? Or tear his poor heart out?"

Before I can answer, I hear my phone buzz and I pull it out to check it. Part of me irrationally thinks it could be a message from "DecOlan," but that's impossible of course. Or Colin, checking to see if I've got my tickets, maybe offering me some backstage passes after all. But it's from someone else entirely. My sister Elena.

ElenaB: enjoy the show 2nite!

KnuckLise99: aw, thanks. dad got me a concert T-shirt. For the BeBopBros! Can u believe him?

ElenaB: seriously? he must be having a senior moment. He got me a rowing sweatshirt from amherst college. Not umass amherst. Where he pays tuition. wtf?

KnuckLise99: lol! should we be worried? early alzheimers?

ElenaB: nah, i just think his new assistant is a screw up.

KnuckLise99: btw, mom's not going senile. turns out she's got a boyfriend!

ElenaB: what?

KnuckLise99: i'll fill you in at head of the charles

ElenaB: it's a plan ;)

The guy behind the Will Call window has black-rimmed hipster glasses and an I-hate-being-trapped-in-this-cubicle scowl.

"Two tickets for Annalise Bradley," I say, and he rifles through his list of names.

And then, he is pulling a small envelope from a little box and handing it over to us. My two golden tickets: floor seats, center section.

"Wow, I have seriously never had seats this good," Maeve says, looking them over. "And you guys are only a few rows away! Cooper must have mortgaged his house for his tickets."

"Don't you dare say anything," I warn. As far as I'm supposed to know, they were comped.

"I won't," she promises. She gestures toward the guys, who are entering the lobby, holding two rolled up T-shirts. "There they are. Let's go."

But I am not done.

"Be there in a sec," I call after her when she turns back to see why I am not coming. She gives me a knowing look, aware of what I am up to, but doesn't say anything, and goes to join the guys in the bag check line while I duck back to the Will Call window.

"Can you, um, do me a favor?" Hipster counter man looks at me warily. I reach in my bag and pull out a bright yellow envelope with the name "Declan" written on the outside. Inside, is a note I have carefully prepared, which says all that needs to be said. A little unfinished business. "Someone might come here, looking for someone. If they do, can you just give them this for me? It's really important."

I try to slide the envelope to him through the slender opening beneath the bulletproof glass window, but he pushes it back at me, shaking his head. "I can't do that," he says snottily through the built-in speaker. "Sorry."

"Why not?"

"It's policy," he shrugs. "We can't be responsible for personal items. Only tickets we've issued."

"Please?" I try asking him again. "I don't know what this person looks like, so I—"

"Sorry," he repeats, looking around me to the customers behind me, who are shifting their feet in annoyance. "Next?"

I stare at him, desperately. This has to work. There is no other way.

I know what other girls would do in this situation. Lean way in, flash a little cleavage. Or, as Maeve likes to say, whip out my weapons of mass destruction. Make them work to my advantage, at least this once. But as much as I'm tempted, I'm just not going to stoop to that.

"Wait," I say, desperately thinking of something else. "Maybe I should call Colin, you know, Colin Dirge, their manager?" I pull out my phone and show him our last text exchange. "We're his personal guests, and maybe he can clear this."

He frowns, looking at the phone and back down at his list, confirming what I am telling him. "Fine," he grunts. He gestures for me to slide the envelope through the slot and stuffs it into his metal ticket box. "Just D for Declan? No last name?"

"Just Declan. Thanks," I say sweetly.

***

Maeve and Declan go in to find their seats, while Cooper and I get in line to buy some snacks. When we are almost up to the counter, Cooper starts to pull out his wallet, but I grab his arm and say, "No, let me. You got the T-shirts, right?" He starts to protest but I insist, knowing it's the least I can do after he probably blew his life savings on tickets.

"So are you a nachos girl?" Cooper finally relents. "Or a chocolate girl?"

"Guess," I say, teasingly.

He eyes me up and down, lingering on my body a second too long. "Salty. Or maybe, sour. You're definitely not all that sweet."

"Watch it," I blush, punching him in the arm, less for the comment than for the once-over.

"What?"

"You know what." I duck my head. We are *not* having this conversation standing in line for nachos.

He still doesn't get it, but his eyes dart downward again. "No, what?"

But I am finally fed up with him playing coy. "This," I snap, pointing to my boobs. "I've had enough with the staring. Yes, I have boobs, but so does every other female on the planet. Yes, they're freaky big, but get over it. My brain is up here. My face, too. And if you can't keep your eyes off them, that's as close as you'll ever get to any of me, ever."

I don't realize how loudly my voice carries, but when I finish my lecture, the entire line is staring at me. And then, a few other girls and women start to clap and whistle.

Cooper's lopsided grin has been completely set straight. "I, uh, g-get it," he says, stammering, his face now bright red. "I'm a jerk. I didn't mean—"

"Yeah, you kinda are," I snap. "How would you like being ogled like a piece of meat all the time? Do you know what that's like?"

He stares at me, floored. "You're right," he says slowly, nodding, as if coming to some decision. "I don't know. But what's fair is fair. I embarrassed you, so . . ."

We have reached the front of the line, but instead of placing our order, he winks at the cashier, "You don't mind, do you, if I just—" and then he starts climbing right up onto the counter. Everyone in line behind us stops talking to gawk at the crazy boy who is now gyrating and wiggling his butt around to the beat.

"Cooper." I cringe. This cannot be happening. "What are you *doing?*"

The entire line is laughing and pointing, and one guy whistles.

He doesn't even seem to be fazed, smiling down at me. "I'm seeing what it feels like. Go ahead, check out the merchandise. I checked you out. Now it's your turn."

"Cooper, stop, please." I want to cover my face with my hands, but I can't look away. I am mortified for the both of us, but at the same time, I can't stop smirking.

"Not so bad, right? Take a good look." The crowd breaks into applause and catcalls, enjoying his outrageous behavior.

When what looks like a manager starts barreling towards us from behind the counter, Cooper quickly jumps down and holds up his hands in apology. "Sorry sir," he nods to the silently fuming manager, then quickly addresses the counter girl in the orange visor. "Two Diet Pepsis, one nachos—and one M&M'S." As she rushes off to fill the order, he leans over to me and whispers: "Don't apologize for your looks. Own it. You're a beautiful girl. But that's not all you are. You're the whole package, okay? Inside and out. And under that hard-as-nails shell, I'm guessing you can be pretty sweet, Annalise Bradley."

He steals a sidelong look at my stunned reaction as I try not to melt. Instead, I pay the girl, grab the box of M&M'S, and return the smile. I may even fish around and find him a green one.

CHAPTER 38

NOELLE

I watch Eva disappear into the sea of bodies, until I can't see her any longer. But I have to let her go. I am here on another mission. I quickly head back inside the lobby to the Will Call window, hoping to find Annalise waiting there for me, that I haven't missed her. But I don't see her there. Disappointment rushes through me. Isn't she coming? Or has she changed her mind? Or had she never really planned to come? Maybe that's it, then. It's over. All over.

I hover in the lobby, uncertain what to do next. I eye the guy behind the Will Call booth and he eyes me back. "Can I help you?" he eventually asks. "No," I shake my head. "I'm waiting for someone." But no one comes. After a little while, when the crowd has all but died out, I hear him calling me. "You. Yes you." He stops and consults something behind the counter. "You wouldn't happen to be Declan?"

I hesitate, then step forward. "Yes."

The guy in glasses gives me a funny look, then pulls something from his box of tickets.

It's not a white ticket envelope like everyone else's—this one is bright yellow. On the outside it says "Declan." He hands it to me and watches me curiously as I walk away to open it. I stop a few feet from the ticket window and tear open the flap. I am confused. Where is Annalise? Why didn't she show? Is this from her? How can I reveal who I am, explain things, give her the VIP pass, if she doesn't come? Did she leave a ticket for me instead, to come and meet her at the seat? But no. Instead, I reach in to find a handwritten note on lined paper tucked inside the envelope. I pull it out, unfold it, and begin to read.

To: "DecOlan"
(OR WHOEVER YOU REALLY ARE)

Did you really think I would forgive you? Why? Because you showed up here in person? Did you really think that an apology would make it all better, after you jerked me around for weeks, played with my emotions, laughing with all your friends at how gullible I was? How I believed all your lies? What you did was sick, twisted, lower than low. What do you expect? That you and I have any basis for a real relationship, after feeding me lies on top of more lies? That anything you told me meant anything? That you can make it up to me? Well, you've come all this way for nothing. Now I hope you know how it feels, to have your hopes raised, to believe in someone, only to be totally humiliated and rejected. Because whoever you are, and whoever you turn out to be, know this: I want NOTHING to do with you. Ever.
  Drop Dead, DecOlan.

Annalise

CHAPTER 39

ANNALISE

The show is about to begin, so I send Cooper ahead to claim our seats, telling him I'm going to the bathroom but will be there soon. Then I sneak back downstairs to the doors just beyond the lobby, peering through at the Will Call window. I have to know. For good or bad, I have to see if he, she, it, whoever, actually shows up. I have to see for myself who DecOlan is.

It doesn't take long. The lobby is practically empty. Except for one person. The minute I see Noelle Spiers standing there, I know. The memory hits me, the phrase she used yesterday, when refusing to tutor me, seemed so familiar: *it's all on me*. It's something "DecOlan" used to say, too.

Everything I know about Noelle comes flooding through my brain as I try to piece together her motivation. Math brainiac. Swimmer. Stuck-up, or so I thought, but maybe just shy. Acute stage fright. Hates attention, kind of like me. We've attended the same school for a whole year, but I can't recall a single real conversation we'd ever had. How does that even happen?

I watch her as she lingers there, waiting. Now, the lights in the stadium start flickering, encouraging latecomers to take their seats, and the lobby empties completely. The man behind the window says something to her, and she tremulously approaches the ticket window. I see her lips moving, nodding, when the man says the word "Declan," then pushes the yellow envelope I gave him through the slot to her. I see her take an uncertain step or two away from the counter, unable to wait more than a few seconds before peeling back the envelope and poking her trembling fingers inside, removing the note I had written. Aware of a deviation from the plan, a trap, she glances around, as if sensing my presence, and I shrink back behind the security guard to make sure she doesn't spot me.

I see her carefully unfold the paper, first one time, then a second, until my words are revealed. She smooths the note on her thigh, then furrows her brow as she begins to read what I carefully printed in hateful black ink.

I wonder how it all started. Did Eva tell her to do it? Did Noelle agree to start writing all those words, and then what? Did she start believing her own lies? That we had a real connection? A relationship? Did we? Didn't we?

And now, what has she come here expecting? Forgiveness? Absolution? Amnesty? After what she did? Really? For me to learn her motivation, hear her apology, clear her conscience for her?

No. As far as I'm concerned, my note says all I need to say.

I turn to go. Unlike Eva, I don't need to sit here and glory in someone else's misery. I have a concert to go to. Cooper Franklin is waiting inside, and Viggo Witts could be coming out any second, and I'm not going to let her ruin something I've been anticipating for so long. Already, I can hear the crowd's hum grow. I can't wait any longer to be a part of this moment.

And then I see it. Dangling from her hand. A precious VIP pass with a lanyard. A pass that allows its owner access to the post-party. To meet Viggo Witts. And I know that it's for me. To make amends. All I have to do is step forward and claim it. It could be mine, if only I could swallow my pride. I want to so badly. But I can't. My hurt is too deep. My trust is too shattered. My forgiveness can't be bought so cheaply. At the end of it all, I'd rather have my dignity than a chance moment with Viggo.

Noelle must have gotten to the end of the letter because she stops reading and looks up again. Even from a distance, I can't help but see the tears streaming down her wet cheeks.

Crying? I want to shake her. Why is *she* crying? She's the bad one here. She's the villain, not me. Eva Winters would never be so weak, would never break down like this. My words were harsh, yes, but nothing compared to what she's put me through. I won't feel sorry for her. I won't. How dare she stand there, making me feel like I'm the monster? She deserves this. She earned this.

I slip away, trying to erase the image of her twisted face from my mind. Stupid me, I thought saying what I needed to say would make me feel better, would somehow even the score, give me closure.

So why do I feel so hollow inside?

CHAPTER 40
NOELLE

I am standing there numb, sick to my stomach at what Annalise had written. Because she is right. Every bit of it. I deserve it. What had I been thinking? That just by showing up here, ready to make my confession, all would be forgiven? That I could wash away my sins with a VIP pass? But, it was just like Eva had said that day at the soccer field. I'd believed because I wanted to believe. I squeeze the piece of plastic in my hand. The gaze of Viggo Witts seems to mock me, his ghostly image appearing and disappearing, depending on which way you tilted him.

I hear whoops and whistles from the audience inside the arena. The show is starting, and fans still lingering rush inside to their seats, leaving me alone, with just the ticket takers eyeing me indifferently.

My phone vibrates. It is a text from my dad, just a big question mark, asking what's taking me so long. Well, that's that. Dad's waiting in the car, and I see no other choice but to go find him. As I turn to leave, I feel someone grab my shoulder. It's Eva, and she looks wild-eyed, reckless. The slit in her dress has torn way up her thigh.

"Come on." She takes my hand and tugs me.

"What? Wait. Where's Amos?" I am almost afraid to ask.

"Screw Amos." And when I look closely at her face, I can see that she has been crying as well. We must look a wreck, the two of us. "He dumped me, okay? For real this time. He's gone. But no way I'm missing my song with the band. So are you coming, or what?"

I don't want to go anywhere with her, and I don't know why she'd want me after I told her we were through, but I numbly follow her past the bag check, into the arena, out of habit, or maybe sympathy, or maybe one last hope of finding Annalise.

I blink as my eyes adjust to the dim lighting, and the brain-thumping roar of the music already pervading the arena. I pull the VIP pass over my head as an usher with a flashlight stops us and checks Eva's tickets, then leads us down, down, down, past rows of jealous faces until he pauses at the front row, right in front of the stage, gesturing to two seats in the center of the floor. We apologetically bob and weave our way past our already-standing seatmates until we find our spots, so close up that I have to tilt my chin and crane my neck to see the singer looming above us.

The spotlights bathe Brass Knuckles in a bluish glow, transforming the musicians into an aquarium of exotic undersea creatures. My eyes sweep the stage as I take in the various band members that, thanks to Annalise, I already know so well: the drummer, Johnny Cape, with his overdeveloped arms and shaved head already shining with sweat; the long-haired bass player, guitar slung low on his hip in a stance of indifference.

Viggo himself commands center stage, dressed all in creamy-white leather, the blue streak in his spiky black hair gleaming dangerously. His face is manly perfection: chiseled cheekbones, square jaw, dark piercing eyes. The music crashes inside my ears and vibrates throughout the rest of my body in waves, obliterating everything else.

I twist and turn, trying to spot Annalise and Cooper, but there's no way I'll ever make them out in the dim arena. We listen, silently, as the band plays one song, then the next. Eva starts revenge-flirting with two guys on the other side of her, trying to see if they are at least twenty-one and will get her a drink. After a few minutes, she is successful, and she downs most of it lightning-fast, laughing to herself, "Liquid courage, right?"

Then she holds the cup out to me, in case I want a sip.

"Beer?"

I shake my head no, remembering that my dad is still sitting waiting in the car, and the smell of alcohol on my grounded breath sure won't go over well. Like he read my mind, my dad texts me again. "I have to go," I tell Eva, but she grabs my hand, pleading, "Not until after my song. You can't."

I sigh, and text my dad back, begging for ten more minutes.

Eventually, Eva starts talking. At first, I don't even realize she is talking to me, because she is staring straight ahead. I hear her mumble something like, "You were right." But those words would never come out of Eva Winter's mouth.

"What?" I shout.

She raises her voice even louder. "I said, maybe this was more about me and Amos than Annalise. Maybe it wasn't entirely her fault. Fine, okay? I get it. So if you have to make amends, whatever."

I am so shocked that she is actually owning up to it, making an attempt at an apology, that I can't speak.

"Did you hear what I said?" Then she finally looks at me and notices my puffy, tear-stained eyes. "Wait, what happened? What's wrong, Noey?"

I try to speak, but can't. How do I tell Eva that I already tried but failed? Annalise will never forgive me, that I came down here ready to grovel, just to have her reject me. But I can't, it is just too loud. Too humiliating. Silently, I hand her the note. She reads it and looks stunned. Hands it back to me.

I expect her to say sorry, to comfort me, to give me a hug.

Instead, she glares at me. "So, you're just going to take that from her?"

"What can I do?" I wince at her harsh words. "She's right."

Eva is angry. But not at Annalise—at me. "Geez. Noey. I thought you'd finally grown some balls. I was actually impressed when you told me off today. That's the first time in a long time you've ever stepped up."

I silently take that in.

"So, don't just take that brushoff from her. If you want to make amends, make amends."

I am shaking my head. "It's too late."

She gets right in my face, grabbing my shoulders with both hands. "It's not. But you're going to have to *make* her accept your apology. Force her to hear you. Show her you mean it."

I want to, but it feels helpless. "How?"

In the background, I hear Brass Knuckles segue into the opening chords of "Identity Crisis." Just then, a huge blinding spotlight shines in my eye. I literally can't see. The white glare freezes me in a hot glow as the crowd cheers, eager for one of its own to be coroneted. A backlit figure is standing high up above us, gleaming, reaching his arm toward us like an angel.

It is Viggo Witts, his microphone tucked under his arm, smiling down at us, out of a crowd of thousands of screaming girls. Suddenly, I feel a hard shove from behind. I am jolted forward, and he is taking my hand, pulling me up stage. I try to tug away, shake him off, tell him he's picked the wrong girl, that he's supposed to pick Eva, of course, not me. But it is chaos all around us, and it is too late. I have been chosen, the Jumbotron has zoomed in right on me, and he is not letting go.

I stumble up onto the massive stage of the Agganis Arena. A zillion darkened faces examine me from a million angles, like a dressing room mirror that shows 180 degrees into infinity. Offstage in the wings, more sets of eyes are piercing me: roadies, musicians, groupies.

"What's your name, luv?" Viggo asks indifferently, and I whisper it into the microphone. Oh my god, that stupid raffle that Eva had to go and win. They must have told him exactly where the winner would be sitting, to pick us out from our VIP passes. But he's somehow gone and got the wrong girl. And Viggo Witts is already gesturing for me to sit on a waiting stool, where I know what will happen next. He will start serenading me with "Identity Crisis," while I sit there. And then—oh, god—he will share the microphone with me and expect me to sing the chorus with him. To actually sing a song in front of an entire stadium of people. Not just that, but people will be filming it on their phones and putting it up on YouTube, where my performance will be immortalized forever. Eva has spent all week practicing, but I haven't. I'm not even exactly sure I know all the words by heart. Compared to reviewing a math problem, singing in a packed arena is like the difference between tackling a rock-climbing wall and scaling Mt. Kilimanjaro.

My head spins with altitude sickness. My body spasms with the bends. And this time, I think it will take my poor pounding heart a million years to recover.

CHAPTER 41

ANNALISE

For the second time in a week, I stand there flabbergasted, as I watch Noelle Spiers—my newfound nemesis—get pulled up on stage instead of Eva, instead of me. What happened? Some mix-up? I look over at Eva, expecting to see her having a tantrum—waving her arms in outrage that Viggo has picked the wrong girl, demanding that security let her get by. But instead, she is standing there serenely, a little smile on her face, nodding encouragingly as Noelle gets pulled on stage.

I might not have noticed it before, but now that Cooper has pointed it out, I can see it clearly: being up there completely freaks Noelle out. She is trembling, literally trembling, as Viggo asks her name and gently gets her seated on the stool. Viggo is perfect, gorgeous, so near I could almost touch him. I will him to look into the audience at me, to give me this chance instead of her. Noelle just sits there, looking zombie-like, or as if she is sleepwalking, awake but not really. I remember the anecdote DecOlan shared about choking at a school concert when he was younger, and wonder if that really happened to her. Is that why she always seemed so stuck-up, when really, she's just super shy?

"Is she going to be all right?"

229

"I'm not sure." Cooper's brow is creased in concern for her. I can feel his anguish. Because he's always going to care about her, I realize, first and foremost, even though he doesn't know it yet.

I think back on all the heart to hearts we'd had, personal stuff, when she'd told me about her dad losing his job and her parents' argument. Was any of it real? Or like she said, was all of it real— except for who she was?

Viggo launches into the band's trademark song, but then, before the first chorus ends, Noelle seems to snap out of her trance. I watch as she rises unsteadily off her stool.

What is she doing?

His eyes squeezed shut with emotion, Viggo doesn't seem to notice her, or at least, he pretends not to. He continues to sing as she inches closer to him.

"Stop," she mouths, and now he gives his head a small, almost imperceptible shake and a frown, as if to say, *don't upstage me, psycho chick.* "Please," she mouths again, and then, incredibly, she yanks the microphone right out of his hands.

Cooper and I exchange a look. *Has she gone mad?*

The crowd starts mumbling and grumbling and the music is still playing, and I can't tell what is going on. Until I hear my name. And I realize that Noelle is speaking into microphone about me. Or to me.

"Annalise Bradley," she says, her hand shielding her eyes from the spotlights as she scans the front rows. Finally, she locates me in the fourth row, pointing at me and repeating my name. "She's the one who should really be up here. Not me. This is her dream, not mine. And it's all I have left, to make it up to her, for what I've done. To show her that I'm truly sorry. To show her that I meant what I said. Every word."

I am stunned.

That she would do this. That she would offer this. That this is really happening. That she is making this happen. If I step forward,

I can take her place up there on the stool, and Viggo Witts will sing to me, and I will sing to him. All I have to do is forgive her. I think back to Elena, and why she said she forgave our father. "Because he got swept up in something he wasn't strong enough to stop. He was weak, I know. But also I know he didn't want to hurt us."

Noelle looks me in the eye. "I know I lied about who I was. I regret it. But everything else about our friendship was true. And all I want is for it to survive." Then she goes on to say she hopes I give Cooper a chance because he really likes me and she's known forever that he's the most amazing guy she knows, but she doesn't deserve him and maybe I do and she hopes we'll be happy together.

Cooper doesn't know exactly what she's babbling about, and gives me a quizzical glance, but it doesn't seem to matter. When she finishes speaking, with a slight crack in her voice, I feel him freeze and gaze at Noelle, like he was seeing her for the first time ever. I can literally feel his crush on me draining away, like a soul leaving a dead body, and rematerializing in a halo of light around her, and although part of me is sad to see it go, another part thinks maybe it is only right.

The audience seems mesmerized, too, staring at Noelle on the Jumbotron, and down on center stage, drinking in every word she is saying, rubbernecking like they are watching a ten-car pile up come to life. They all crane their necks to see who she's talking to, and who this Cooper guy is.

But here's the weird thing: The whole time she's talking, even though the microphone is in her hand, even though Viggo Witts is standing right there, gaping at her like a goldfish, you can hear his silken voice, still oozing from the speakers, loud and clear. And it feels like all of sudden, the entire stadium's attention shifts back from Noelle to Viggo and collectively notices that pesky little detail.

And that's when the proverbial you-know-what *really* hits the fan.

CHAPTER 42

NOELLE

Everyone—and I mean everyone—is staring at me, but for this brief, exceptional moment, I totally don't care. I have put it all out there. What I did. How I feel. What I want. The only one I am watching now is Annalise, sitting there next to Cooper in the fourth row. Viggo just stands there, dumbly, when I finish talking. The music is about to launch into the final verse of "Identity Crisis," the one he and I are supposed to sing together. Annalise still hasn't made a move. I can't tell if what I said has made a difference. Not knowing what else to do, I plead, "Come on, Annalise," and I start singing along. Well, singing would be generous. Wailing badly is more like it. I manage to remember the words to the final verse.

"You see me, and I see you
But perception can be so untrue
I'm having an identity crisis
Why'd you have to leave me to my own devices?"

And then I see her whisper something to Cooper—will she?—and she leaves her seat and clambers tentatively up onstage to stand beside me.

Our eyes connect. But before we can say a thing, the audience's murmurings have turned into outright boos and yells of outrage. For a minute, I am confused. Why is the crowd so angry? Did I mess up the song that badly? Did my stunt ruin the concert? Then I realize what everyone else has already figured out: Viggo Witts's voice is still wailing alongside mine, even though I am the only one holding the microphone.

Viggo Witts isn't singing live at all.

Viggo Witts is a big, fat, lip-synching fake.

I turn to see Viggo staring at us in disbelief. For a second, I wonder if this has all been some mistake. If the silver-tongued singer will come up with some excuse, sweet talk the hostile crowd into loving him once more, and start the song all over again, this time serenading Annalise exactly as she has always dreamed.

Instead, he glares hot lava at the two of us and bolts off the stage.

Annalise and I look at each other, like, did he just do that? And holy crap, what now? And if you thought the crowd was crazy mad before, you should really hear them now. They are Tahrir Square pissed, and hostile cries of "faker" and "poser" and "loser" fly through the air. Even though we are not technically the object of the anger, I'm scared we're going to be pelted with empty Pepsi cups and nacho cheese if we stay up here much longer. The rest of the band doesn't seem to know what to do; they just start playing a long riff over and over again.

Annalise stands slack-jawed; her stunned gaze follows Viggo as he disappears into the wings. I feel sorry for her—it's like she has finally grabbed the brass ring on the carousel, only to find it made of rust, crumbling in her hands. And it's partly my fault.

She turns back to me, the only one left. "I can't believe it. Can you?"

But I can. Because I know how Viggo feels. I have been a faker, too. And I'm not alone. It seems everyone has something they are covering up—an aging face or a crumbling career, a secret crush or a true identity. We're all just a bunch of glamour shots and Facebook brags and auto-tunes. What feels real can turn out to be fake, but also, what feels fake can sometimes turn into something real. All that flashy gadgetry—our handles and avatars and screen names—can let us scrape away the surface and connect somewhere true, somewhere deep inside. At least, it did for me.

"I'm so sorry," I tell her, hoping she has found a way to forgive. For what I did to her. For what Amos did. For what Viggo did. For everything.

I watch her face carefully, to see whether she will nod and accept my apology, or shake her head and refuse it. But before she can do either, the lights in the arena are suddenly snuffed out. We gasp and blink as a blanket of darkness envelops us. For a moment, it is pitch black. A voice comes on the sound system, asking the crowd to remain calm, assuring us they are experiencing "minor technical difficulties" and the show will resume "as soon as possible"—all words everyone knows are a blatant lie.

For a moment, I am freaked, standing there feeling so small, so alone, even in a packed stadium. I know Annalise is standing right next to me, and though I can't see her, I can feel her presence. Then a few emergency exit signs pop on, shining like lighthouse beacons in the far distance. People in the audience start pulling out their cell phones, to text or chat or just illuminate the blackness, and soon, it's as if a thousand tiny stars flicker all around us, pointing the way. Annalise's fingers reach out in the dark, seeking mine, and then our hands clasp tightly. She leans in, gently takes the microphone out of my other hand and whispers in my ear, "ready for an encore?" I squeeze her hand back, hard, the tension flowing out of me, and tell her I am. Our connection is strong and true and real, and for the first time in a long time, I no longer feel alone in a crowd.

EPILOGUE

ANNALISE

"Hurry up," I tell Noelle, as I practically drag her down the stairs of the musty Harvard Square coffeehouse. "Colin swore we wouldn't want to miss this." We feel our way down a dimly lit hallway where we are stopped by a burly bouncer wearing a black T-shirt. "Ten bucks," he demands, holding out his hand.

I pay the cover charge for both of us and we slip inside the room, past a poster advertising tonight's performer: "Drew Tangier"—an ugly, aging hipster gripping an acoustic guitar. I'd gotten a cryptic text from Colin Dirge a few days ago, tipping me off that I might be interested in catching a show by this no-name up-and-comer.

I've learned not to ignore these tips.

"You swear the lights aren't going to go out this time, right?" Noelle asks, teasingly.

Things did get freaky-scary that night of the concert, when the Agganis Arena lost power and the rest of the Brass Knuckles' show was abruptly canceled. Luckily, Noelle's dad was waiting right outside in the parking lot and gave all of us a ride home, especially since my mom was still out on her date with Gerald. Who knows if they'd still be together if I'd screwed up their big romantic dinner that night?

Of course, the label's publicity machine went into overdrive, claiming that Viggo was just using his own pre-recorded vocals as filler to preserve his voice in concert, like so many pop stars do. That worked, until rumors began circulating that it wasn't even his voice at all, and he hadn't even done his own vocal work on the album. By the end of it all, the head of the music label was forced out, Brass Knuckles had to return their Teen Pick award, and the arena was forced to refund everyone's money for that night's show, which meant at least Cooper got the money to buy back his beloved baseball card. Maeve made sure I didn't miss the cover story in *People* magazine where Viggo tearfully confessed that spontaneously erupting nodes on his vocal cords were forcing him to retire from the music industry, but he would be pursuing a film career in Hollywood instead.

I'd assumed Colin would be furious with me for my part in exposing his client as a fraud, but from the comments he made in interviews, he seemed strangely Zen-like about the whole thing. Relieved, almost. In a roundabout way, he'd even tried to warn me that day at the mall not to get too attached to Viggo Witts, hadn't he?

I had sent him a one-word text—Sorry—but never heard back and figured that was that, until a few months later he texted me out of the blue, saying he was starting up his own label and inviting me to join a street team of teen music scouts. Our job is to go listen to live performances by artists that he's considering signing and give him feedback. Sweet! He even pays me a stipend, which is going into my boob-reduction fund, although I'm no longer entirely sure I'll ever go there. I'll have to wait and see.

If I do change my mind, I've got an easy way to score the cash: a set of VIP passes for the Brass Knuckles' final concert are going for, like, seven hundred bucks on eBay. Noelle thinks I'm crazy for hanging on to it, but I like to take it out sometimes and play with the hologram label, just to remind myself of the things that are real, and things that are an illusion. Besides, give it a couple more years, and those puppies could fund my entire college tuition bill.

"Where's Cooper?" Noelle asks anxiously.

"Relax. He'll be here soon."

It wasn't hard to see the two of them made the perfect couple. Maybe he'd been blinded by my boobs for a while, but it's clear the two of them are made for each other, and I'm not going to let possessiveness over some guy mess up a friendship again. Noelle's old posse is gone. Tori's parents transferred her to some fancy boarding school in Connecticut, and Eva is spending spring semester in Los Angeles, filming a TV pilot. Noelle claims that there is some redeeming value in Eva, that she willingly gave up her shot in the spotlight—but I'm still not convinced Noelle didn't mistakenly end up on that stage from a random shove. We'll have to agree to disagree.

"Is Maeve coming?"

I sigh. "Don't ask." Maeve has been sucked into Declan's weirdo homeschooling crowd, spending her weekends on citywide scavenger hunts and tromping through graveyard tours. I tried talking them into meeting us here, but they're off at some Medieval Faire, garbed in authentic period costumes and salivating over turkey legs.

The waitress comes by and Noelle orders a pair of lattés for us. "On me," she says as usual, happily pulling out a bill from her wallet. Ever since her dad started up his own private accounting practice, she has been on a serious caffeine high. I feel slightly guilty, considering all the free math tutoring she's given me, but she insists.

Cooper finally arrives, sliding into the seat Noelle and I have saved for him. "You're late, Franklin," I bark. "Lost your way?"

He smiles back, knowing I am just messing with him. "I know you said underground, Bradley, but I didn't realize you literally meant subterranean," Cooper jokes back, then grabs Noelle's hand protectively. I roll my eyes, keeping them trained on the stage, as the lights dim and Drew Tangier shuffles out, clutching his acoustic guitar. He is sporting an enormous set of bushy eyebrows, and for a minute, I can't imagine why Colin insisted I come. Rock star? This guy? The next Viggo Witts? No way.

Cooper is clearly thinking the same thing. "You sure this is your man?" he asks me, eyebrows raised. "Your taste in musicians is dubious, I think we've established."

"Don't start," I tell him, although I'm wondering the same thing myself. But I've learned the hard way to look deeper, to disregard the shiny surface, as tough as that can be. And then, it is clear why Colin has sent me here. As soon as the singer opens his mouth, I know exactly what I'm about to hear: a silken voice so familiar I would recognize it anywhere.